MERRYMAN'S CROSSING

•

Ellen Gray Massey

AVALON BOOKS
NEW YORK

PRINTED IN THE UNITED STATES OF AMERICA
ON ACID-FREE PAPER
BY HADDON CRAFTSMEN, BLOOMSBURG, PENNSYLVANIA

To my sisters, Kathryn and Gertrude:
Thanks for being there all my life.

Chapter One

Stunned, I jerked upright. I almost fell off my folding chair in the crowded office when the lawyer finished reading the last section of my grandparents' will. Did I hear him correctly? My grandparents left the store to me and expected me to move back to Merryman's Crossing to run it!

Earlier, while the lawyer had been reading through the preliminary legalese in his monotonous drone, my mind had wandered back to memories of childhood summers with my grandparents at their country store. I sat quietly and inconspicuously in the corner with my brother as the lawyer was explaining various legal points in the will. He explained about Dad and Uncle Bruce being the personal representatives, and that the bulk of our grandparents' assets would be divided be-

1

tween them. He paused and then announced that there were four special bequests.

"The first bequest, and the most important one," he said, "is to Kay, contingent on her accepting it." He turned to me. I was suddenly thrust front and center. Yes, I heard him correctly. The store might be mine. The pleased faces of my family smiling at me proved it.

"Oh, my goodness!" Mom said in delight and reached across Dad to squeeze my hand.

"Wow!" came from my eighteen-year-old brother, Dwight. He poked my arm gently with his fist to show his delight.

"Good deal, Kay," my cousin Merl said, sending me his congratulations across the room.

"How wonderful!" Aunt Betsy said. Uncle Bruce grinned his agreement and nodded his head rapidly.

Dad and my uncle exchanged pleased glances. "Bruce and I have been worrying what we'd do about it," Dad said. I could tell the bequest took a load from him, for neither he nor Uncle Bruce had time to manage the store.

Lowell Boyd smiled at me. I hadn't noticed that he had a charming lilt to his eyebrows when he smiled. But then I probably hadn't seen him smile because I'd just learned at the service who he was, a nearby neighbor of my grandparents. But I had no clue why he was included with our family at the reading of the will.

"Pearlie Kay." I hated when Dad called me that baby name. "You will accept it, won't you, Pearlie

Kay?'' he begged; the sadness in his face since Grandpa and Grandma's double funeral had lifted.

Immediately the atmosphere in the room changed from sorrow and loss to cheer and hope. Each member of my family grinned happily at me. Though gone, my grandparents' bequest focused our thoughts on the future and not on our loss. My acceptance would reunite the family and ensure the continuation of a century-long Merryman family tradition.

The words of Grandma's favorite hymn rang in my head, ''Will the circle be unbroken?'' She and Grandpa were assuring that it would stay intact. But the decision rested with me.

I was too stunned to answer Dad. Overwhelmed is a better word. Thoughts darted through my head so rapidly, I couldn't control them—happy childhood vacations with my cousin and little brother at our grandparents' store, my present satisfactory life as a writer, and my family's enthusiasm. Mingled with thoughts of my family was an awareness of Lowell Boyd's keen brown eyes evaluating me from across the room, and Dwight's body tensing up whenever he looked at him.

What was with this guy? I didn't know anything about him, and I couldn't figure him out. Dwight obviously disliked him, yet my grandparents respected him enough to include him in their funeral. The words and melody of the last line of his original hymn that he sang at the service still rang in my head: ''And the union of souls with those gone.''

Was ''gone'' the operative word? Or was it

"union"? During the service all I could think was that my grandparents were gone. Now, hearing their wishes and seeing the happy reaction of my family, I realized they weren't really gone. I took a quick glance toward Lowell Boyd. He had pegged it correctly. It was a reunion.

When Dad couldn't take my silence anymore, he repeated, "You'll take it, won't you, Pearlie Kay?" I still had no answer. I continued to ignore him.

Heav-vy! My intuition that my life would change when I said goodbye to Grandpa was right on the mark. The change would be about-face, no less. Everyone in the room was hanging onto my answer, urging me to say yes to the bombshell the lawyer had just dropped.

"Your grandparents, Kay," he had read from their will, "if you so accept, bequeath to you their store at Merryman's Crossing, the building and its contents, the adjoining old school building, the old blacksmith shop, and the hundred and sixty acres surrounding them."

He had paused, but we knew he wasn't finished. We waited for the rest. "And twenty thousand dollars cash to make any needed improvements or changes that you want to make right away." He hurried on, ignoring the comments and exclamations from most of us. "This bequest depends on your willingness to run the store yourself for at least five years."

Even with everyone in the room watching me, anxious for my answer, I prolonged my silence. I needed to think through the recent happenings before I could even consider giving any answer. I reviewed what had happened since my quick trip home from Kansas City when I had heard of my grandmother's death, followed less than two days later by Grandpa's. I had arrived just in time for the double funeral.

At the funeral service I couldn't place the tall, handsome soloist listed on the leaflet the funeral director handed us as Lowell Boyd. He looked familiar to me, and obviously meant a great deal to the family. He was probably one of the neighbors I used to see when I visited my grandparents on the river at their big white building that was both store and dwelling. I'd been out of touch with my home county since I went away to college, and after graduation I had lived in the city.

I wondered about him. He sang an original hymn in his deep bass voice. My parents and aunt and uncle were moved by his tribute. On his way back to his seat among the pallbearers, he had clasped Dad's and Uncle Bruce's hands and nodded to Merl, Dwight, and me behind them on the second row. When Lowell Boyd looked at Dwight, he almost frowned. Dwight's body stiffened. Even then I sensed the animosity between the two.

Dwight's hostility came to a head when he, Dad, Mom, and I were ushered into the lawyer's private office half an hour ago. My uncle and aunt and cousin Merl were already there. Seated beside Merl and in deep conversation with him was, not his fiancée, Vivian, whom I halfway expected, but Lowell Boyd!

Dwight had halted at the door so quickly that coming behind him, I almost collided with him. "What's he doing here?" he blurted out when he spotted Lowell. Before anyone could answer, he turned, pushed me aside, and ran out.

"What's the matter?" I had grabbed his arm, surprised at this sudden anger from my usually happy-go-lucky brother.

"I can't go in there with him!" he said.

I didn't know what the trouble was between those two, but I did what I could to avoid a scene at the reading of my grandparents' will. Noticing the anguished looks on Mom's and Dad's faces, I pleaded with my brother, "Please, Dwight, come on in. We'll sit over here away from him." I took his arm and pulled him to a couple of folding chairs across the room from Lowell. Dwight sat there with a scowl on his face during the entire time the lawyer was explaining the will.

The lawyer had droned on about some legal points and then looked up at the family gathered around him. "Dwight, Kay, and Merl," he said, "in this will of your grandparents, they made several specific bequests. One to each of their three grandchildren." Dwight and I glanced at each other in surprise. We assumed that everything our grandparents owned would be divided equally between Dad and Uncle Bruce.

"And one to Lowell here," the lawyer said.

I kicked Dwight's leg to warn him to keep quiet. "You may be surprised to learn," the lawyer continued, "that your grandparents were well off. Their estate is sizeable. All their lives they lived frugally and saved, investing wisely and carefully in land and stocks, mostly mutual funds. Your grandfather asked me to amend his will from the original one that divided their holdings between his two sons. He said that he and Faith had worked it all out together. This is what they both want and what we finalized."

He paused to be sure everyone was with him. We were, because we all knew that while Grandma lay in the funeral home, Grandpa came to town to finalize his business. Then he went home and lay down for a nap from which he never awakened. They were always together; I could picture my grandparents even now walking happily hand in hand down a shining path.

"Before the assets are divided," the lawyer continued, "he specified that four separate bequests be distributed. The first one is to Pearl Katherine Merryman, commonly known as Kay." He spoke directly to me. "The last thing Olen said when he left my office was, 'Tell Kay that I hope she will, but she doesn't have to.'"

"That's what he kept saying to Merl and me just before he went to sleep," Dwight said. "What did he mean?"

"He meant that this bequest, like the three others I'll explain directly, is contingent on her willingness to do it.'' He paused and cleared his throat. ''Since this one involves so much more than the others, Olen wasn't sure that they were doing the right thing. But he said he and Faith had studied on it for a long time. They talked about it and both thought that it was what they should do. But they didn't want to force Kay in any way. She shouldn't feel obligated or experience guilt if she chooses not to accept it.''

He spoke as if I weren't there, using ''she'' instead of ''you.'' He continued, ''They both believed this would be a way to insure having what they value so much continued and preserved, and at the same time to give opportunities, experience, and happiness to their only granddaughter.''

''Do what?'' I asked. ''What is it that they want me to do?'' Accepting this bequest would mean a complete change of life from my part-time job at a convenience store in Kansas City while I struggled to be a freelance writer of historical fiction.

How could I make this life-changing decision on the spot? Dad and Uncle Bruce would surely sell the store if I didn't take it. And who would buy an out-of-date country store, anyway? But that century-old family store couldn't just vanish! That was unthinkable! My grandparents knew that no one else in the family would, or could, run it. I was the only one with retail experience.

''Well, Pearlie Kay?'' Dad asked, bringing my thoughts back to the present.

"Don't rush her, dear," Mom said. "Give her time to think about it."

"Good idea," the lawyer said. "I'll continue with the second bequest." He shuffled through his papers and picked up the correct one. "To his grandson, Merl Merryman, goes fifty thousand dollars specifically contingent on his marrying Vivian Coffey, whom he has been dating for several years, and using the money to build a house on the five-acre piece of land he owns just south of town. Faith and Olen believed that the reason Merl and Vivian haven't married is that neither has enough to start out with." He looked up at Merl, and from my cousin's happy face I knew that this part of my grandparents' will would be carried out. "He believed that with both Merl's and Vivian's skills, the money would be enough that they could build themselves an adequate house. Merl could build it, and Vivian decorate it."

"Vivian should be here," I said.

"I tried to get her to come," Merl said, "but she didn't want to intrude on family affairs."

Dwight nudged me and cocked his head toward Lowell. His lowered eyebrows indicated, "Then why is *he* here?" I shrugged my shoulders and shook my head slightly to caution him to keep still.

"Now Vivian'll be family," Aunt Betsy said, patting Merl's knee.

"Can we be there when you propose?" I teased him. "Family business, you know."

Merl's crinkling up his face warned us that we were excluded from this.

"The next bequest goes to Dwight Merryman." The lawyer took up another sheet of paper. "Dwight, your grandparents specified an equal amount of fifty thousand dollars for you."

Dwight flinched and gasped. We all smiled at him.

"It is to be put into a trust fund," the lawyer continued, "handled by your sister, Kay. The funds are to be used only for some advanced education beyond high school, not to pay off debts or other obligations. The wording doesn't specify college, per se, but some training toward preparing you for a career. When you finish the course of study, and this is to be determined by the trustee, who will be Kay, any monies remaining and the interest thereof will be given to you to do whatever you wish when you are twenty-five years old. But, until that time, if you get into any further trouble with the law, the entire trust will be given to a charitable organization of Kay's choosing."

He paused. No one said anything. I was flabbergasted. I had no idea what Dwight thought. And what was this about trouble with the law? I shot a glance at Dwight, who avoided meeting my eyes. The lawyer continued speaking to Dwight. "This money is to enable you to further your education while working part-time to pay off your fines. Your grandparents at first named your dad and mother as the trustees, but decided on Kay because she, being of the same generation, will be better able to judge whether you have met the requirements of the trust. In other words, they thought she would be more lenient and, if I may say, more forgiving of youthful escapades.''

What youthful escapades? What fines? Dwight continued to avoid eye contact with me. He kept his eyes fixed on the lawyer.

Dad and Mom both smiled and nodded. ''That she would,'' Dad said.

''Good choice,'' Mom agreed.

''Now, Dwight,'' the lawyer continued, ''you don't have to accept this bequest. Just like Kay's getting the store, if you don't accept it, then the amount will go back into the general fund to be divided between your father and uncle.''

''I accept,'' Dwight said almost breathlessly. Every person there, including Lowell, smiled. Dwight made the right decision. Grandpa and Grandma certainly knew what they were doing.

''Good,'' the lawyer said. ''Now as to the reason Lowell Boyd is here.''

At the mention of Lowell's name, Dwight rose to his feet before I could stop him. ''I can't stay here,'' he said to me as he dashed out the door.

Dad gave Mom a hopeless glance and followed him.

''What's the matter?'' I asked Mom. We both stood up.

''Just a little trouble between Dwight and Lowell,'' she whispered. ''Sit down, dear. He'll be back.'' She sat down and patted an empty seat beside her for me. But her expression belied that the trouble was ''little.''

No way could I sit down. "Mr. Hansen," I said to the lawyer, "would you please excuse us for a few minutes? We'll be right back."

The lawyer laid his papers down. "Sure. We'll take a break."

I followed Dad and Dwight out into the foyer.

"I won't," Dwight was saying, very much like the little rebellious boy he used to be.

"You have to," Dad said.

"No, I don't. He's the one who has to go. He's not our family. What's he doing here, anyway?"

"Grandpa asked specifically that he be here."

"I don't care. I won't go in."

Dad turned to me. When we were growing up, I could usually manage Dwight when our parents couldn't.

"What's this all about?" I asked.

"Dwight got into some trouble and Lowell . . ."

Mom joined us. "It was just a silly, boyish prank," she said, "but Lowell didn't think so. He talked to the judge and . . ."

"And the judge put me on probation, and I have to pay humongous fines." Dwight's face was livid. He clenched and unclenched his hands. "And here he is in the center of our family's private business where I can't look anywhere but see his self-righteous face."

"Come with me, Dwight," I said, taking his arm and dragging him toward the outside door. "Let's take a walk. Mom and Dad, go on back in. We'll come in a minute."

Surprisingly, everyone obeyed me. When Dwight and I were out in the street walking rapidly down the block, I said, "Tell me, Dwight. You know I'm always on your side. What's this all about?"

We walked another half block before he calmed down. "All right, Kay, but I hoped you wouldn't ever have to know this. Just before graduation some friends and I decided to have some fun. The other two guys knew of this guy who had a Harley that he hardly ever rode. He always kept it covered up with a tarp in his garage that was out of sight from his house. One of the guys thought it would fun to ride around in it— show off, you know. So we loaded it in his old pickup, took it to town, and we joined the crowd cruising around. I'd never been on a motorcycle, so one of them drove it, and I sat behind him."

He saw my horrified face and rushed ahead before I could butt in. "We were going to take it back, honest, Kay. Just a little joyride. I know it was dumb, but we didn't hurt it. Went, maybe, four or five miles, tops. But someone recognized the Harley and notified the owner. He called the sheriff."

"No one told me anything about it."

"No, no reason for you to know."

"Is that what Grandpa was talking about in the will about trouble with the law?"

Dwight nodded.

"What happened? How did Lowell Boyd get into it?"

"We were charged with felony theft, and breaking

and entering. The other two guys were sixteen and as minors weren't charged, even though they were the ones who started it and took turns doing the driving. I was just along for the ride. But I was charged as an adult. For a while it looked like I'd have jail time. Grandpa made my bail and got me a lawyer—not that one back there, but one who specializes in kids' cases. The man who owned the Harley pressed the maximum charges and claimed we damaged his cycle and caused him mental distress. Because I was a good student and an Eagle Scout, and had never been in trouble before, my lawyer first thought she could get me off with just a small fine. But Lowell,''—Dwight's voice tensed— ''he got involved. He's county commissioner, you know. . . .''

''No, I don't know. I don't know anything about him.''

''Well, he is. He just got elected last fall on the platform that he would stamp out robbery and such stuff. He has lots of clout. He talked to the judge. The judge put me on probation for six months and slapped on a huge fine that I must pay myself, and in addition, I have to pay the owner restitution for his potential damage and his 'distress,' the judge called it.''

''How much?''

''Three thousand total.''

''Pretty steep.''

''Yeah, and relatives can't pay it for me. I have to earn it myself and present receipts to prove that I did.

The judge set up a payment plan. First is due June thirtieth.''

''Wow!'' That was a pretty heavy burden to pile on a kid just out of high school. ''But why would Lowell talk against you if he is such a good neighbor to Grandpa? Looks like he would help you.''

Dwight's next words came out so garbled that I had to listen closely to understand him. ''Because he doesn't approve that his sister and I date. . . . I mean, dated. He put a stop to that.''

''Why didn't you tell me?''

''Didn't want you to think bad of me.''

''Oh, Dwight, I'd never think that.'' I pushed him lovingly. ''You're my pesky little brother, but no one can hurt you without dealing with me, right?''

''Yeah, but I thought it was time I fought my own battles.''

''I'm proud of you.'' I could tell that wasn't the response he was expecting. ''I'm proud that you are handling this yourself. So, c'mon. Ease up on Lowell. Time will pass; probation will be over. You've got a new job at the factory, haven't you?''

Dwight nodded.

''That will help you repay the money, and if this sister of Lowell's . . . What's her name?''

''Shannon.''

''If Shannon is what you think she is, she'll be your friend again. Right?''

Dwight smiled. ''I guess. She still writes me notes that she leaves . . . left . . . with Grandpa at the store.''

"See, I know I'm right. Don't you worry then. She still likes you. Now you be the bigger man and go back to face this Lowell Boyd, County Commissioner, who abuses his power over high-strung but loveable high school seniors." Dwight laughed. "See, he's nothing but a bully."

"I guess."

"C'mon. Dad and Mom have been through enough the last few days. Don't add any more. Your trouble is history. Past tense. Let it be and look forward. Okay?" I stopped and looked him straight in the eye. He could never resist me when I did that.

"Okay."

We slipped back into the lawyer's office and sat down in our chairs. All eyes were on us as I nodded to Mom and Dad that things were under control. "Sorry about the interruptions, Mr. Hansen. Please continue."

I cast a quick glance at Lowell. He seemed unperturbed, chatting with Merl and Uncle Bruce. When the lawyer cleared his throat, ready to resume, everyone quieted.

"The last bequest is to Lowell," Mr. Hansen said.

"Cool it," I whispered to Dwight. "Grandpa must have had a good reason." I put my hand on his leg as if I could control him by my touch.

The lawyer continued, "As you all know, Faith and Olen have had a long tradition of encouraging music. They were very proud of their neighbor, Lowell Boyd, and what he has done with his own music. Therefore,

Olen instructed me, if Lowell is agreeable, to set aside thirty thousand dollars in a fund to help any person in the county who wishes to study music. This can be in private lessons or at a recognized institution. And he wanted Lowell to be in charge of that, investing the money and paying it out at his discretion as long as it lasts.'' He turned to Lowell for his answer.

''I would be proud to handle that request,'' Lowell said. ''I am honored that they would name me.'' This was the first time I'd heard his speaking voice. It was deep and as musical as his singing one.

So this was why Lowell was included in our family meeting. I felt some of the tension release from Dwight's leg. Apparently he didn't object to this bequest. Not a bequest, exactly, but a responsibility my grandparents asked Lowell to take on for them and for the community. It made good sense. Continuing with the music business was something the family didn't have to worry about. I was glad.

Mr. Hansen gathered up his papers and stacked them neatly. He was finished. Everyone agreed to the terms of the will, and Merl, Dwight, and Lowell all accepted their special bequests. That left me. I still hadn't given my decision.

Everyone looked at me. I'm always uncomfortable being the center of attention. This time was worse than usual. So much depended on me. Dwight was smiling, his fury gone. Merl, Uncle Bruce, and Aunt Betsy nodded at me, urging me to say yes. Mom's lips formed the word, ''Please,'' though she did not voice it. Even

Lowell was sitting on the edge of his seat, looking expectantly at me.

Dad's eyes were begging me. "Pearlie Kay?"

"I don't know. I'll have to think about it some more," I said. Dad smiled in relief. At least I didn't say no. "But, Dad, I've got a restriction on it, also. If I accept, it will be only if you promise never to call me Pearlie Kay again."

Chapter Two

It was like stepping back in time when I walked around the antique gas pumps early the next morning to climb the two steps onto the wide porch across the front of the large wooden building. Above the porch roof, between the upstairs windows where the living quarters were, was printed in large, though faded letters: MERRYMAN'S GENERAL STORE. Under it in smaller letters was MERRYMAN'S CROSSING, MISSOURI, followed by the zip code. Against both walls, under the windows on either side of the center door were worn, backless benches.

Would this be my future? Back here in this out-of-date Ozark store instead of the fast-paced city life I'd enjoyed for the past few years? Grandpa and Grandma seemed to think so.

Dwight had told me that Grandpa wanted to tell me

something. "Tell Kay that she doesn't have to if she doesn't want to," he had told Dwight just before passing. I know now it was about the store. He didn't want me to take it if I didn't want to.

I'll always be sorry that I was out of touch with my family. Even irresponsible Dwight had lectured me about that. "You should let people know where you are," he said in a newly found mature voice. This was unusual talk from my harum-scarum younger brother, who was always getting into mischief and rarely showed consideration for others. It was always I who fussed at him to behave.

But I was so elated over the terrific book contract I'd just signed, I had grabbed my laptop and taken off on a research trip, one step closer to my long-range goal of being a full-time writer. My book would be the first in a series of historical novels for young readers that a New York publisher was producing. If I finished it in three months, I'd have a shot at writing others in the series. I was so deep into the records of French fur traders in the St. Louis courthouse that I forgot everything else.

Now, I wondered as I studied the old store building framed with oak and hickory trees, could I handle this business and my writing? My grandparents must have thought so, for no way would they do anything to hinder my writing career.

"Howdy there, young lady!" I jumped at the husky voice that banished my wandering thoughts and brought me back to the reality of the porch at Merryman's Store. I hadn't noticed an old man grinning at me from a bench at the far end of the porch. He was dressed in blue overalls, gray chambray shirt, and battered straw hat. Expertly, he closed his pen knife and slipped it into his pocket. On the floor in front of him was a small pile of shavings from the stick he held in his hand.

"Hi," I said, wondering if by some magic I had truly been transported back sixty years. Since I didn't see any car, I assumed someone must have dropped him off.

"You Olen and Faith's granddaughter?" he asked, rising and walking toward me.

"Yeah, I'm Kay."

"Olen said you'd likely take over the business. You've growed up some. Last time I seen you, you was . . ." He held his hand about three feet from the porch floor. "You was only so high."

"I'm not sure yet whether I'll take over, but I'm opening up the store today. Can I help you with anything?" I hoped he wanted bread or some other staple that I could find quickly. I had driven down from Mom and Dad's early, so I could look around before any customers came.

"Naw, just enjoyin' the sunshine this fine June mornin'. Chet and Steve should be here directly. Surprised they ain't come yit."

"Do they need to get something?"

The man, who appeared to be about Grandpa's age, shook his head. "Naw, we jest set here most good days. Sun ourselfs in the summer and come inside outta the cold in the winter."

"Enjoy yourself, Mr. . . ." I said when he sat back down and resumed whittling.

"Clyde," he said. "Clyde O'Quinn, live just up the road a piece. Next place beyond the schoolhouse."

When I opened the door, a potpourri of odors greeted me. In addition to the usual smells of a store, I detected the smell of leather, new denim pants, shoes, and dress goods mingled with the fragrance of brown sugar, spices, vinegar, tobacco, wood smoke, and dust from the many feet trampling over the wide, bare boards of the floor. On the left, where the old-fashioned upright cash register sat on a worn, smooth wooden counter, were the groceries. Across the wide center aisle, broken by racks of potato chips and other modern snack foods, and believe it or not, a black woodstove and a few ladder-back straight chairs, were bins of hardware supplies, such as nails and screws. Along the back aisle were bolts of cloth and sewing materials.

In one corner there was a nook containing a bench and a few worn chairs beside shelves of magazines and paperback books. In the opposite corner was the post office, a counterlike window that was closed now, behind which were cubbyholes for the patrons' mail.

In the back, hidden behind the refrigeration units

filled with soft drinks and dairy products was the narrow stairway that led upstairs to the living quarters. I
knew I'd have to go up there where my grandparents
had lived since their wedding day over sixty years ago,
but not now. Dad and Uncle Bruce would come later
to go through their things and take what they wanted.
My job today was to see to the store. I had agreed to
run it for a week before deciding whether I should
accept it.

I heard voices from the porch. Clyde's cronies must
have come. They poked their heads in the door to
wave at me and welcome me. A young woman, obviously on her way to town to work, rushed in for a
diet soda, a grape pop, and a package of doughnuts.
''Sorry about your grandparents,'' she said. ''Hope
you won't close the store. We need it. Oh, by the way,
I'm Maria. I live a half mile on up the road beyond
the O'Quinns.'' Without waiting for my reply, she ran
out, greeted Clyde and his friends in a cheery voice,
handed the can of pop to her little boy in the backseat,
and drove off.

For the next few hours a steady stream of people
came in to get their mail, buy a few supplies, or just
out of neighborliness and curiosity. The regular customers showed me where things were and patiently
explained how to operate the cash register, the post
office, and other details of my grandparents' business.
Their system soon came back to me, the one-on-one
service and precomputer accounting that hadn't
changed since my childhood days of helping out.
Quite different from standing behind a secured counter

passing items over the bar code reader in the convenience store in Kansas City.

Sometimes the customers picked up the items they
wanted and brought them to the counter, but some read
from a list as I gathered the things up. Everything was
done the old-fashioned way. I remembered that
Grandma used to write each purchase down on a
ticket. More recently they used an adding machine. I
remembered Dad saying that he gave it to his parents
one Christmas when Grandma complained that her ar-
thritis bothered her so that it was hard for her to write.

I soon developed a system to keep up with the customers. I couldn't believe there would be so much
business in this little store umpteen miles from no-
where. I also took mental notes of what I might do to
make things easier, or of commodities I might add to
improve sales. Though at first annoyed at the lack of
modernization, I began to see it as an asset. I was
included in the conversations around me as a person,
not just a fixture behind the counter. I noticed the
change in people's demeanor the moment they stepped
through the screen door. Each one, even the hurried
young woman, Maria, who stopped to grab an un-
healthy breakfast, slowed down and relaxed in the old-
fashioned atmosphere. Noon came before I realized
how quickly time passed.

"Is every day as busy as this?" I asked a talkative
lady who was recounting how glad she was that I was
keeping the store open.

"Oh, the store has lots of business. Maybe more

today because ever'body is wanting to see you."
Boldly she looked me over from my short, tossed hair
to my sweatshirt, blue jeans and jogging shoes.
"Faith, your grandma, she asked me to help you out.
Why just last Sunday evenin' when I come in, she was
restin' over there on her chair." She waved her arm
in the general direction of the book nook. "I see,
Olen's taken it out. Well, just last Sunday she told me
you'd need some encouragin'."

"I appreciate it. I need all the help I can get." I
pointed to a young couple with a child. "They aren't
from around here, are they?"

"Land sakes, no, child. They come off the interstate. Some folks do now since they opened up that
new access ramp last summer."

"How do they know the store's here, across the
river and on this country road? It's not even on the
state highway."

"The signs the highway department puts up at every
exit on the interstate. You know, them big blue rec-
tangular ones that show what's available, food, gas,
lodgin'. There's one there for Merryman's Store
showin' the gas symbol. That brings a few, but some
folks turn around 'cause they don't know to turn off
on this road. They can't find the store. And those that
do see our road, lots of people don't like to drive
through the water on that low bridge or travel on
gravel roads."

During a lull at noon, I fixed a sandwich from the
grocery supplies, and popping a soda can, I went out

onto the porch to flop onto a bench. That was the first time I'd been off my feet all morning. I had the store to myself. Clyde and his cronies were gone. I propped my weary feet on a nail keg, sipped the soda, and let out a big sigh of relief. If I took over the store, I'd never have to worry about gaining weight. I understood how both grandparents kept so trim.

I should sweep up the shavings, I thought, but for the moment all I wanted to do was sit. The breeze coming around the building blew a few shavings onto the ground. When I tipped the can up to get the last liquid, I noticed a little figurine on the window sill behind me. Though crude, I recognized that it was a replica of me! The clothes and even the harried expression cut on its face were mine. It was standing on a slip of paper. Scrawled in pencil was "It'll get easier."

I laughed. I ran my hands over the figurine, feeling its smoothness where Clyde had shaved it carefully around the body and the roughness of the cuts that formed its base. It was so perfect that I cried, weary from my hectic schedule—the week researching in St. Louis, the rushed trip home, Grandpa, Grandma, this impossible store, all the nosy and wonderful customers. My roots were strangling me. What of my own future as a novelist? I should be working on my story about the fur traders that I had partially planned out in my mind. "Why did you have to go, Grandpa? You really put me into a bind."

I heard again the words he told Dwight to tell me,

"You don't have to if you don't want to, but I hope you will. . . ."

I promised Dad I'd give the store a week, but one morning almost finished me off. And then I found this absolutely perfect figurine made just for me by a man I didn't know! Perhaps my roots were protecting me.

Across the country road that paralleled the river, a blacksmith shop and a bank of trees blocked the view of the water, though if I listened carefully I could hear it lapping against the rocky bluff.

To my right, down a little hill, the road narrowed to one lane as it forded the river and joined the tarmac on County Highway M. Perhaps forded is not the correct word, because there was a concrete bridge with flanges leading to it from either bank and six-inch curbings on the edges of the runway to prevent the vehicles from going over the side. However, the bridge floor was at normal river level. Much of the time, water ran across it. Accustomed to it, local people easily drove through the few inches of water.

From straight ahead, across the river and about half a mile farther on, I could hear the semi trucks on the interstate highway. To my left, next door to the store, stood the old stucco one-room school building. Kept in good repair, it had been the community gathering place since my grandparents bought it in the 1960s when it closed. A bit farther on was a house, probably Clyde's home. Behind the buildings were the hilly and rocky woods, all 160 acres of uncut and untamed

Ozark upland. The river curved around the acres, roughly forming their western and northern borders.

Not used to the continual hum of motors from the interstate and thinking so hard about my situation, I didn't notice the sound of a single pickup truck approaching from my left. It pulled up to the gas pump. Since the pumps were not self-service, I quickly wiped away my tears, slipped the figurine into the front pocket of my sweatshirt, and reluctantly rose from my seat to wait on the customer. The driver was obviously a nearby neighbor, for he had driven with practiced skill down the rough country road that dead-ended a mile and a half south of the store.

"Hi," said the deep voice that I recognized before I saw the tall man himself.

"Hi yourself, Lowell," I said. "How much you want?"

"Fill it up. But I'll do it." He grabbed the hose just as I was ready to thrust it into his tank. "Most of us go ahead and get the gas we want and then come in to tell Olen or Faith how much it is. Saves them having to trot out here all the time."

I noticed he spoke in the present tense, as had many of the customers during the morning. Everything indicated my grandparents' presence. And apparently people accepted me as their extension. The talkative lady had even said that I resembled my grandmother when she was my age.

"We did what we could to help them," Lowell said, unconsciously slipping into the past tense. "Sometimes when Faith had one of her spells and stayed upstairs, we'd just get what we needed and leave the money on the counter.''

I couldn't believe such honesty and trust. In the city at the store, we had all kinds of security measures, and even with automated gasoline pumps and the checkout counters positioned right by the door, people managed to cheat in many ways.

''What if people don't tell the right amount, or just drive off without paying?''

''Never used to happen. It does some now, though. I'm working to put a stop to all the stealing and pilfering that is increasing in our county.''

I looked at him to see if he was speaking about Dwight's case. Apparently not, for he continued in the same general tone, ''Since the new ramp was put in up there for access to Highway M,'' he pointed toward the interstate, ''there've been more problems around here. I tried to get Olen and Faith to install automated gas pumps and alarm systems, but they wouldn't hear of it. But I'd advise you to do so.'' The gasoline machine clicked off. He replaced the dripping nozzle and screwed down his gas cap. ''Olen said that would probably be one of the first things you would do.''

He was about the fifteenth person to tell me what my grandparents said to them about me taking over the store. Each time I became more disturbed. ''Everyone in the county seemed to know they were giving me the store. . . . except me.''

''Not everyone. None of your family knew. Olen

and Faith decided on that part of their will just a few days before she died. It was only then that Olen confided in some of his regular customers to encourage them to keep shopping here.''

''And he told you?''

''Yes. Olen talked with me about it. He also discussed with me the music fund they set up.''

''So that wasn't a surprise?''

''No.''

I couldn't help being a bit peeved that he knew things about the will before my family did. Grandpa and Grandma must have really liked him. Then I thought of what he did to Dwight. I couldn't understand this man.

We walked back into the store, and I rang up his gas purchase. ''How did the morning go?'' he asked. His eyebrows lifted with his rare smile.

''Fine. I've had lots of experience running stores and waiting on people. I just had to learn the ropes here. This is like another world.'' I put out my arm to indicate the open kegs of eight-, ten-, and twenty-penny nails, and the jars of cellophane-wrapped red-and-white-striped stick candy standing on end in round jars with lids. There was the huge circle of American cheese lying on a worn wooden stand. A homemade butcher knife lay beside a V-shaped chunk already cut out. ''It's like being transported back to the early 1900s.''

''Yeah, cool, isn't it?''

I hadn't thought about it that way. I laughed, "Yeah, it is cool."

"People like it this way. Olen and Faith knew you would make lots of changes; that's why they added the extra money so that you could, but they hoped you wouldn't remake it completely to look like any modern convenience store."

"Everyone just assumes that I will stay."

"Yes. We all hope that you will. At first I wasn't so sure, but I watched you yesterday, and from the talk of the neighbors on the telephone this morning, I think you'll do."

Though I resented his checking up on me and evaluating me, I kept a pleasant expression. "I told Dad and Uncle Bruce that I'd give it until next Friday. By then I'll probably know what to do."

"Good move. Any more thoughts now after this morning?"

I had been putting together in my mind what people said to me and my own ideas. "Yes, one main one. The neighborhood trade is good and is probably the steady income that supports the business, but I think I see a way of increasing that."

Lowell's eyebrows contracted into the frown I detected whenever he looked at Dwight. It was as if he knew what I was going to say and he disapproved. "How?"

"By enticing more people off the interstate. Advertise the authentic country store angle. Keep all the trappings, like the pot-bellied stove, the rustic post office, and wide porch with old men whittling, but add some tourist-type stuff. Maybe home-canned food, local crafts. Stuff like that.'' I pulled Clyde's figurine out of my pocket and set it on the counter. "Like this.''

Lowell looked at it as he said, "Couldn't you do that without bringing people off the highway? Couldn't the local trade and that from town do the same thing?''

"Not dependable enough. People here don't think that stuff is worth buying since they see it all the time. The store where I work in Kansas City gets seventy-five percent of its income from tourists and truckers coming off the highway. Yet it was first designed as a neighborhood store. There we could sell lots of carvings like this one Clyde did this morning.''

We walked out onto the porch again into the balmy June air. Lowell looked at me with respect. "Nobody ever thought of selling Clyde's whittlings. He makes something every morning. Faith used to complain about having to continually sweep up after him.''

"I think his whittlings would sell. And I bet there are other men and women in the neighborhood who could make some extra money with things they make. Help out the store, too.'' I couldn't understand why Lowell was still frowning because my plan would help out the local people as well as the store. He walked down the steps to his pickup.

"But before I could draw much business from the highway,'' I said, looking toward the river, "something would have to be done about that low-water bridge.''

The frown on Lowell's face became a scowl. ''Forget that,'' he said in the tone of voice he had probably used to cause Dwight so much trouble. No wonder my brother disliked him so much. His manner changed abruptly from a friendly, neighborly advisor to an authoritarian who knew his power. ''That bridge stays just the way it is.'' He stepped up into his pickup, and without looking back or saying more, pulled his door shut.

His back wheels spewed out gravel when he revved his engine and sped down the hill. Scarcely slowing, he hit the water that was flowing almost level with the six-inch curbs on the concrete bridge. Waves of water sprayed on both sides of his passing, like Moses parting the Red Sea. Across the bridge, his red truck dripped water, leaving wet black tracks in the gravel as he disappeared around the bend. The sound of his motor became a steady hum when he reached the paved highway, momentarily blotting out the continual background noise from the interstate.

''Don't mind him,'' said a voice behind me. I turned to see the talkative lady whose information about the sign on the interstate first started me thinking about the possibilities of the store. ''He means well, child, but he's too full of his own importance. And short-sighted. All of us livin' on this road, except him, want a good bridge down there.''

''You surprised me. Do you live close by?''

"I live just up the road. Walked over. Your nearest neighbor. Nora O'Quinn. You probably don't remember me, but I remember you comin' to visit those summers. How Faith and Olen doted on you!"

"Is Clyde your . . ."

"Yeah, he's my man. We don't do much no more. Retired, you know, 'cept for a few cows and a couple of old sows. Livin' off our savings and Social Security now. But Faith and Olen, they wouldn't quit. They jest kept on a-goin' even though they had plenty of money and was older'n us."

She stepped up the stairs to the porch as quickly as me. "I jest come back for some vanilly. I started to bake Clyde a birthday cake and saw I was out of flavorin'. He's eighty-one. I'm eighty," she said proudly.

"You two sure don't look it."

I took a bottle of vanilla off the shelf and rang it up. She counted out the money from a worn, snap coin purse she pulled out of her apron pocket. "Don't waste no bag on me," she said, slipping the bottle and coin purse into her pocket.

Since she didn't seem to be in a hurry, I asked, "Why doesn't Lowell want a new bridge? Being county commissioner, he could get it, couldn't he?"

"Yes, he could. And he can also block the bridge petition. That's what he's doing."

"So you've tried to get a new bridge?"

"Yes, but it's been turned down."

"Did my grandparents try to get a new bridge?"

"They didn't care one way or the other. When they

seen there was disagreement in the neighborhood about it, they let it go. Didn't want to stir up no hard feelings. But—'' Nora leaned forward and lowered her voice—''they told me that you would see to it that we got the bridge once you took hold here.''

This was getting scary. My grandparents anticipated every thought I'd had that morning about improving the store. Even from the grave, were they programming me? No, that wasn't so. Grandma and Grandpa always let me do what I wanted and make my own decisions—even wrong ones. When Dad and Mom wouldn't let me do something, they would. But about this bridge. I reasoned that they simply knew me so well that they didn't have to guess what I'd do. My family!

Tears welled to my eyes. My roots were creeping around me. I didn't know whether to break loose from them and continue my struggle to become a successful novelist living in a big city or let them enfold me back to my family and home county.

''We're all broken up, child,'' Nora said, putting her hand on my shoulder and patting it. ''They leave a big hole in the neighborhood and in our hearts. We're all taking comfort that you are following them. You'll do just fine.'' She started toward the open door. ''Call me if you need anything. The numbers of all the neighbors are there by the telephone behind the counter, and upstairs in their living room.'' She looked at Clyde's figurine prominently displayed on the counter, then back at me and smiled. "My goodness, Clyde and me, we're glad you're here."

When I reached the door to watch her leave, she was striding rapidly past the old schoolhouse toward her house on the hill, on the same road down which Lowell had recently driven his truck on his way to the store.

"How much for this cute little statue?" asked a woman who was looking around the store while Nora and I talked. I turned back to her. She was holding Clyde's figurine.

"Oh, that's not for sale."

The women pursed her lips in disappointment. "It's really cute. Can you get me one like it? I pass through here every week. Could you have one for me next Friday?"

"I don't know. I'll see."

Reluctantly, she set it down and gave me a five dollar bill for the snack food she bought.

I didn't have time to savor how right I was about selling local crafts because two cars pulled up outside. I was very busy the rest of the day.

Chapter Three

All during the rest of the week the neighbors gave me all sorts of encouragement and help. They just assumed I would stay. Without my asking, Nora and Clyde explained in detail how my grandparents ran the store. They told me the schedules of the regular salesmen and their individual idiosyncracies. They expounded on the uncertainties of the mailman who delivered the mailbag for Merryman's Crossing post office. It seemed he often did not cross the bridge when the water ran more than a few inches over it. This was a sore point for them, as they depended on their papers coming in the mail each day.

"If the river gits just an inch over the four inches he thinks is safe," Clyde said, "the regular mail carrier honks and waits for Olen to meet him across the bridge to get the mail bag. But on the days the substitutes run the route, they don't bother. They just skip us that day.''

Clyde's friend Steve, after watching a tourist pick up one item at a time to bring to the counter, suggested that I get little carrying baskets that could hold all the purchases at once. To prove his point, the next day he brought me a handwoven white oak basket he had made. ''Here, Kay, set it on this here little stand by the door so people will pick it up. They'll buy more stuff if it is handy for them.''

Supermarkets had discovered the marketing device of using carts years ago, but Merryman's Store was too small and crowded for carts. Its customers didn't buy large quantities at a time, just three or four items at most. ''Baskets are just the ticket,'' said Steve.

''Yeah,'' Clyde agreed. He was thrilled that his whittlings were selling. I had sold five for him in two days. ''And when you ring up the stuff, you can ask them if they wouldn't like to buy the basket, too.'' The two men poked each other to punctuate how astute they were.

The idea worked. The first day I set the three baskets out, a commuter from the interstate bought one of them.

During the week other neighbors gave me ideas. One time after I filled the gas tank of a tourist family, the young boy was fascinated with the ancient unused gas pump Grandpa never got around to removing. When the boy asked how it worked, Chet stepped down from the porch and sauntered over. He pointed to the markings on the glass holding globe on top of the pump.

"Young feller," he said, "see them lines that show the gallons? When the level drops, you can tell how much gas you've put in your tank."

He put the child's hand on the lever on the side of the rusting shaft. The gears groaned and squeaked as the delighted boy cranked the lever back and forth, pretending he was pumping gasoline into the glass tank.

"Cool!" the boy said, grinning. He ran back to his father, chatting excitedly about his new adventure.

"I could fix this pump up," Chet said to me as we watched the sleek van creep down the hill, pause at the low-water bridge, and inch across the water so slowly that hardly a ripple of the river flow was disturbed. "I could connect it to the holdin' tanks under the new pumps." He studied the pump, walking slowly around it. "All it'll take is some rust remover, a bit of paintin', and some oil in these here old joints. And scourin' out the glass. It'd be good as new."

"Why would I want to fix it?" I asked. Then I understood what he was suggesting. An operating antique gas pump would give the store still another link to the past, sort of a beacon to draw people. "I could probably charge more for gas from the hand-operated pump, couldn't I?"

"Good idea. Then let people, like that young'un there, do their own pumpin'," Clyde said.

"Might be worth a shot," Chet said, becoming in-

terested. "Wouldn't cost much to try. I'll get right on
it fer you." He didn't look to see if I agreed. It was
as if we were all in this together.

Nora had told me that before Chet retired, he
worked with iron in the tool and die factory in town.
As I turned from the pump, I glanced across the road
at the boarded-up building that used to be a blacksmith
shop. I wondered if the forge and anvil were still there
as they were when Merl and I used to play there as
kids. Wouldn't it be something to have a working
blacksmith shop again? I wondered if Chet would be
interested.

These ideas and others of my own flooded my mind.
I was developing a daily routine and devising ways to
save my energy. I was becoming acquainted with the
neighbors, the postal patrons, and other regular customers. Maria, the young mother on her way to her
baby-sitter and to work as nurse's aide in a rest home,
stopped every morning for her drinks and something
sweet to eat. I thought, *Why not put in a coffee pot
and hot cocoa, and offer some nutritious pick-up food
for breakfast?*

Clyde, Steve, and Chet were morning regulars. Nora
and a couple of other neighbor women who lived farther up the road always came in the afternoon, right
after washing their noon meal dishes. Lowell stopped
by twice during the week for gas. Once when he was
on his way out, the next time when he was coming
home. Though he was always in a hurry, he chatted
for a few minutes, mostly about how I was getting

along, and offered help if I needed it. One time he helped me move a counter back to make more room in the reading corner. Another time, when it took me a while to find his mailbox, he suggested I organize the boxes with labels.

"Olen and Faith never installed the lock boxes the post office sent them but kept on using these cubbyhole slots. They knew without looking where everyone's mail went." Before the week was over, I knew, too.

People who lived south of the store on Highway M stopped in less frequently, usually on their way home from working in town to pick up some bread, milk, ice cream, or soft drinks. "You should carry beer," one of them said. "Faith wouldn't hear of it, but a young woman like yourself, you wouldn't care."

Not a bad idea, I thought, but I was with Grandma on that. Young woman or not, I didn't want that. No beer.

Then there were the people from the interstate. Surprisingly, there were regulars from there, too—truckers, salespeople who had regular routes, and commuters to or from Springfield.

I could always recognize the first-timers. They entered hesitantly, as if they had stumbled into a time warp. Assured of the store's reality when I greeted them in modern cut-off jeans and sweatshirt, they stared at the interior in amazement. If there were any children, their parents pointed out details in the store just like those they remembered from their childhoods.

Invariably the black stove with its pan of ashes underneath drew the most comments. "All you need is a spittoon," one man said, staring unbelieving at the stove.

Even the children were awed, behaving as if they were in a museum. They tentatively put their hands out to touch the jars of striped candy, expecting me or their parents to tell them not to touch. "Would you like some?" I'd ask. They always nodded their heads. I made a sale.

Sometimes the uniqueness of the store was a liability. People asked innumerable questions and delved into long discussions about their own childhood experiences in country stores. I'd listen with one ear, while trying to wait on someone else.

One time when I was really busy, Nora happened to come in, this time for a box of "baking powders." She always bought only one thing at a time. I soon realized that gave her more excuses to come to the store. She diverted the customer's attention, and listened and explained while I helped the next customer.

When the store was empty again, Nora explained, "I thought you might need some help. After Faith got too weak to wait on people herself, she would visit with the customers so Olen could keep up."

Then there was Lowell's sister, Shannon. She and I hit it off right away. She'd look through the magazine section first. Then she would read the blurbs on the books from the bookmobile that stopped by monthly to see if she wanted to check them out. Or she would prop herself on the old bench to read the daily papers.

"You should put in a video rental section," she said. "We're too far from town to rent videos and have to take them back the next day. If you had them here, we could rent much oftener." She presented her library card to check out a book. "Or even better, have a movie at the schoolhouse every Friday. Give us something to do besides joyriding."

When she realized what she had said, she clapped her hand over her mouth, embarrassed.

"Is that why Dwight took the Harley?" I asked. "Bored for something to do?"

"Those guys in town talked him into it. He said something to them about this old man and his Harley Davidson just setting there, no one using it. It was their idea to borrow it. Dwight was with them, and he just went along. I don't really know why. That isn't like him."

"I know it isn't."

"But Lowell won't listen. He won't let me see Dwight or have anything to do with him. He thinks Dwight is part of a gang, or something."

"So I understand."

"He isn't. Dwight is the sweetest, kindest . . ." she paused to find other suitable words to express her feelings.

"He's the best," I finished for her. I agreed because, after all, he was my brother.

"Yeah. How can we make Lowell see that?"

"We probably can't," I said. "Dwight has to somehow prove Lowell's wrong. I think he's starting out right with his new job. He seems much more mature."

"I'll be eighteen this summer. Lowell can't tell me what to do after that. I'll be an adult and full partner with him on our ranch. I'm not a kid. He better understand that." She laid the correct change for a candy bar on the counter. At the door she paused and said, "Think about showing movies at the schoolhouse, maybe on alternate weeks with the music parties. It'd bring in more business from kids around here."

Even though the neighbors and customers were full of advice, my family was unusually quiet. They said nothing to me about the store, though normally they freely told me what to do about everything. They offered suggestions about the upstairs living quarters, what I might want or not want in the way of furnishings, but they left me entirely alone in the store. Dad popped in one day to buy some items. Uncle Bruce offered to clean the ashes from the stove, and once Aunt Betsy volunteered to sweep out, but I was ready to lock up and declined their help.

The store was to be mine if I wanted it. Since there was no mention in the will of partnership with any other family member, they must have agreed among themselves that the best means of persuading me to stay would be to do or say nothing. I was the store expert.

Their tactics worked. Their unspoken words and the silent pleas in their expressions were more potent than any amount of advice and persuasion. Was that strategy part of my grandparents' plan also?

On the first Sunday, staying at the store to save the twenty-mile trip twice a day from town, I even had time to work on my novel. In the quiet of the living quarters, overlooking the lush hillside of oaks and hickories, the rocky ground coated with ferns and mosses, I found that ideas and words came easily. I completed ten pages of my first chapter and had rough notes for the rest of the action.

I centered my story around an Osage boy living near a trading post in the Ozarks. The story wrote itself as I gazed at the rough hillside. Even the thin stream of mist I saw rising up from the hill in back of the store gave a touch of mystery and intrigue to the setting. Stepping into the kitchen for a drink, I looked out the window overlooking the road and the line of trees bordering the river. Absolutely perfect. Clyde had even hinted at some stories handed down in his family about their friendship with the Osages before the tribe was moved to Oklahoma in the late 1800s.

When the week was up on Friday night, the family was all there in Grandma's living room upstairs from the store. Dad and Uncle Bruce had spent several hours during the week sorting through Grandpa's things and taking away items that they wanted or that I would have no use for. Mom and Aunt Betsy did the same with Grandma's belongings. After loading the last into Uncle Bruce's truck, the four of them relaxed on the sofa and easy chairs they thought I should keep.

Merl and Vivian, all excited about their upcoming wedding and plans for their new house, were looking at blueprints spread out on the table in the adjoining kitchen/dining room.

"It's just so perfect," Aunt Betsy said to them, "you two marrying here where your grandparents lived their lives."

"Yes," Uncle Bruce said. "Dad and Mother were born two months apart on these two neighboring farms. They went to that schoolhouse together." The tears in his eyes were not because he was sad, but proud that his son was carrying on in his parents' tradition.

"They were together even in death," Dad said with pride in his voice.

"Like them, Vivian and I have known each other all our lives and went to school together," Merl said, putting his arm around Vivian. They came into the long living room and joined the group.

"And I hope that when our time comes, we will go together like Faith and Olen did." Vivian fondled Merl's hands—hands that could make anything, play several musical instruments, and put together the intricacies of the electronic equipment more rapidly than anyone else in the factory where he worked.

"But that's a long way off," Aunt Betsy said. "Let's think about your wedding, which Faith and Olen have made possible."

We heard the unmistakable rattle of Dwight's old car on the gravel outside. Hurrying down after the afternoon shift of his job at the boat factory, he pulled his old car beside Uncle Bruce's loaded truck and jogged from the private parking space across the leveled-off lawn to the main door of the living quarters. The first floor of the building, the store part, faced the road. But being built on a hillside, the entrance to the house was in the back.

"Have you decided yet?" Dwight asked me as he bounded in.

Everyone was there because my trial week was up. No one was sure what I'd do, even I, though all during the week everyone had been making plans as if I would stay. Mom and Aunt Betsy had discussed which of the furniture and household goods they should leave for me to use. Dad and Uncle Bruce discussed whether I would need Grandpa's pickup; without asking me, they decided that I'd need it for getting supplies for the store.

Dwight had asked if Shannon could continue leaving notes for him at the store where Lowell wouldn't intercept them. Merl and Vivian planned to have their wedding in the old schoolhouse for their mid-July date.

"Well?" Dwight asked during the pause when everyone was looking expectantly at me. "Next Sunday shall I go with you back to Kansas City to get your stuff?"

"Merl and I will help you unload it," Vivian said.

"You may borrow my truck," Uncle Bruce said.

"The store's pickup might not be big enough to haul everything in one trip."

"You don't have to give notice at work, do you, dear, since it is only part time?" Mom asked.

"One thing at a time," Dad said, moving his hand back and forth to stop the questions. "Let her speak." Everyone became quiet and looked at me. "Kay." He pronounced my name distinctly and paused dramatically to show me that he was honoring his part of the deal. He wouldn't call me *Pearlie* Kay. "Kay?"

I was outnumbered, outmaneuvered, and outflanked. I had been by the store's customers all week and now by my family. And most especially by my late grandparents. I was surrounded, encircled here in their living room where Grandpa lived his entire life and Grandma lived since the day they married, and where they both died. Their presence was everywhere, even though many of their things were removed. The Merryman family circle was complete when I fell into the empty chair beside Dwight. Vivian's presence was a normal extension of the family. As members are subtracted, others are added.

Before I could answer Dad, Lowell, and Shannon knocked on the open door and entered when the chorus of voices invited them in. Dwight and Shannon exchanged quick, happy glances before looking away.

"Sorry to intrude," Lowell said, "but we are just getting home and saw all your cars here." He turned to me, "We wondered what you've decided since the week is up."

"She's just about to tell us," Dad said. He pulled a couple of folding chairs out of the closet. When Merl and Vivian scooted together to make room, he set them up by the door across the room from Dwight and me. "Here, sit down. Glad you're here."

No one had to urge Lowell a second time to join the group. "I need to know as soon as possible," he said as he sat down, "to decide what to do about the music gatherings at the schoolhouse. There's one coming up soon."

I could stall no longer. My trial week was over. Merl grabbed Vivian's hand. Dwight and Shannon looked at each other boldly for Lowell was watching me closely, nodding his head slightly, encouraging me to say yes. Dad started to say something, but Mom shook her head at him. He closed his mouth and sat motionless.

I had no choice. I really never had from the moment the lawyer read aloud my part of the will. I knew it then; the week just sealed the lock. "Okay," I said almost under my breath.

Everyone was silent, expecting me to say more.

"Okay what?" Mom asked.

"Okay, I'll stay."

All spoke at once. Lowell jumped up and started across the room toward me, but Mom beat him to me. Dwight and Merl clapped me on my back. Vivian hugged me, as did all the other women there. When Lowell reached me, he stopped, slightly embarrassed, as everyone could tell that he intended to hug me.

Instead he held out his hand, grasped mine in his strong grip, and shook it, giving me his special smile.

Behind him Dwight and Shannon did a high five, and then clasped hands. Dwight whispered something to her. She looked at me, grinned, and nodded to Dwight.

"I'll call the lawyer," Uncle Bruce said, going right to the telephone. "I'll tell him to get the papers going right away. He'll have to see about a merchant's license, about transferring the post office to you, and everything to make it legal. . . ." We couldn't hear the rest of what he mumbled about the store's not having to close.

When he returned from his call, he looked from me to Dwight. Then at Merl and Vivian, and last at Lowell. "We got the ball rolling." He clenched his hands in his enthusiasm. "Everyone has accepted their special bequest just as Dad and Mother wished, so first thing Monday morning, he'll get things moving. Merl and Vivian have already started on their house plans and set their marriage date. Congratulations, son!"

Merl and Vivian beamed when everyone else expressed best wishes. "July twenty-four," Merl said. "Is the schoolhouse free then, Lowell?"

"Sure is."

"Good," Uncle Bruce said, beaming at Merl. "That'll be a happy event."

We all agreed.

Uncle Bruce continued, "Dwight's planning to enroll in the state university for the fall term. His new job at the factory this summer will help him earn enough money to keep up his payments on his fines.''

When I saw the worry lines leave Mom's face, I knew Dwight hadn't told them his plans. Nor had he told me. I had been so busy with the store and my own decision that I hadn't thought much about my responsibility toward Dwight. As soon as the money would be available from his trust, I'd need to pay his tuition.

''And Lowell,'' Uncle Bruce continued, ''has already made arrangements for three young people to take lessons, two on the piano and one on the fiddle.'' We all smiled at him. ''Anything else, Lowell?''

''Now that Kay will keep the store as is, I'm ready to go ahead with plans for the annual county-wide musical at the schoolhouse next month.''

''Very good.'' Being the eldest member of the family now, Uncle Bruce was taking his role very seriously. ''Everything seems to be progressing nicely.''

''Just like Grandpa and Grandma planned it.'' Merl said out loud the words I was thinking.

We all sat silent for a few seconds, thinking about Olen and Faith.

''I brought a cake,'' Mom broke the silence. She hurried out to her car for it.

''I'll get some ice cream from the store,'' Dad said, starting to go downstairs. Then he stopped. ''Is that all right, Kay? I'll leave the money on the counter.''

''My treat.'' I laughed.

Vivian and Merl fixed some instant lemonade.

"What would you have done," Aunt Betsy asked Mom as they were cutting the cake and putting slices on plates, "with the cake if Kay had said no?"

"I'd feed it to the fish in the river." She laughed.

"But you were pretty sure of her answer, weren't you?"

"No, not a hundred percent sure. She's pretty head-strong and won't be pushed. I thought she would, but I wasn't as certain as Olen and Faith were."

Shannon and Dwight sat side by side at the kitchen table to eat their refreshments. Lowell's expression soured when he looked at them, but he said nothing. Shannon didn't look at him to give him an opportunity to object. Maybe knowing that Dwight was being responsible was softening his attitude toward him. Or more likely, he didn't want to make a scene in my house while we were celebrating. I caught my breath. I had thought *"my" house*.

During the week Nora O'Quinn had told me that Lowell had been Shannon's legal guardian since their parents' deaths several years ago. They lived on the family stock ranch at the end of our road, where Shannon did as much work running the ranch as Lowell did. Shannon was enrolled in Drury College for next fall. The college is not far from the state university in Springfield. No wonder Dwight was so happy with our grandparents' trust for him.

I sat beside Dwight with my slice of cake. "I thought you might want to go to Drury College since Shannon is going there," I said to my brother.

"I thought about it. I'd like to, but the university has more possible majors. I thought I might major in agriculture." I didn't say anything but was puzzled at his choice. He grew up in town and knew nothing about farming. When I remembered Shannon's interest in the ranch, I understood. "And the state university doesn't cost as much," he added.

"But Grandpa's trust would probably cover the cost of a private college."

Dwight shook his head. "There wouldn't be anything left over. I'm going to pay off that fine as quickly as I can. Then I'll probably keep a part-time job to have as much of the trust left as possible to have something to start out with."

Smart thinking. I didn't have to worry about my kid brother anymore. He had his head on straight. I thought his problems were smoothing out for him until I saw Lowell scowling at him and Shannon. Dwight glanced at Lowell and whispered to me. "Besides, Lowell would go ballistic if I went to the same college as Shannon. He'd probably send her to Vassar or someplace in the East. This way we're in the same city."

Though Lowell chatted with Dad, Uncle Bruce, and Merl, he was constantly aware of Dwight's attentions to Shannon. *Give him a break, man*, I thought. *They're just kids trying to become adults.*

When Lowell noticed me staring at him, his appearance changed immediately. He smiled; the tilt of his eyebrows made his face radiant and disturbingly handsome. My decision to run the store obviously pleased him.

I'd never been this confident before, this important, and this needed. Momentarily, I was king of the mountain (or rather, queen). My world had righted. I no longer felt the emptiness from the death of my grandparents. I would always miss them, but I wouldn't mourn them. I was happy for Merl and Vivian, and for Dwight. I was content with my decision to stay in this extraordinary store. It was my choice, not the family's or community's, but what I wanted. The possibilities were endless; my future seemed rose-laden. How could Grandma and Grandpa have been so astute?

I looked at Lowell and could hear again the lovely melody he sang at their funeral. When I tried to remember the words, I realized they were more hopeful and inspirational than sad.

"Lowell," I asked him, "would you sing again the song you wrote for my grandparents?"

"Oh, would you?" Mom asked.

"What a lovely idea," Aunt Betsy said.

"I'll run out to my car to get my guitar." Merl jumped up without waiting for Lowell to agree.

Pleased and smiling, Lowell sang. Everyone in the room listened with rapt attention, including Dwight, who tried to cover his appreciation of the song with his frown.

"I call it 'Our Last Good-byes'," Lowell said.
Merl played an introduction and Lowell sang:

When we come to the foot of the hill,
When we see the sun set in the skies,
When we wade through the one final
    stream,
It is time we must say our good-byes.

The true love of us all through our lives
Has prepared us for heaven's domain.
But on earth we still mourn our deep loss
While rejoicing in heaven's great gain.

So we need not show grief for those gone,
Whose long lives full of love are now done.
The dead days of their trouble and toil
Are now lost in the greatest reunion.

For our life on this earth will soon end.
To get ready for life from now on,
God's eternal reflection of love
And the union of souls with those gone.

The last line replayed in my head as Merl strummed
a few closing chords. "And the union of souls with
those gone."

"Gone" is a relative term. No one is truly gone;

new people are added, and younger ones continue the work of those before them.

I was no longer an observer in the background, vicariously living other people's lives in my stories. My grandparents had thrust me into the mainstream where I was making things happen. I was living.

I'm scared, Grandpa.

Chapter Four

A month later, when Lowell picked up his mail after filling his pickup with gas, he wasn't in his usual high-spirited, don't-waste-any-time mode. He popped the lid of a soft drink and took a long swig of it before slapping a twenty-dollar bill on the counter. "Ten-fifty-eight for gas," he said. But instead of standing impatiently as he usually did while I rang up the sale and counted out his change, he straddled one of the split-bottom straight chairs by the stove, so he could face me. He sat down with a sigh, sipping his drink in obvious pleasure. "Hot out there," he said. "Feels good in here. Your new air-conditioning unit is a great addition."

"I sure like it," I said.

"So do your customers. Maybe they'll hang around in here out of the heat and buy more stuff."

"Yes," I said, "That's the whole idea."

"County court has recessed for the summer," he said. I couldn't tell whether he realized my strategy was working on him. "Been a busy session. I've got some free time now."

During the month I'd seen him frequently, though briefly each time. He would run in with his gas money, grab something quick to eat, and dash out again, barely saying more than hello.

His sister, in contrast, spent leisure time with me every day when she came at noon for the mail. Sometimes dressed in her jeans and boots, Shannon would ride her mare the mile and a half down the road to the store. Now during summer vacation and when Lowell was busy at the courthouse most days, she ran their ranch, checked on the stock, repaired fences, and other chores. During haying she directed the workers and drove a tractor to cut and bale their many acres of hay to winter their cattle.

She started eating her lunch at the store after I put in a miniature delilike section with frozen sandwiches customers could heat up in my little microwave. I added fresh fruits and some desserts, like pies and cakes. I discovered that the salesman who delivered ice cream could supply me.

But this day was a first for Lowell to spend any time in the store. He gazed around with interest at the changes I'd made and nodded in satisfaction that while bringing in new commodities, I hadn't materially altered the old-fashioned air of the store. Popping in as he had been doing, he hadn't noticed my gradual changes. Now, relaxing with his drink, his arms resting on the back of the chair he straddled, he noted not only the deli counter beside the refrigeration unit and the bakery display, but the rental videos and Steve's baskets. In addition to making the baskets available for customers to gather supplies, I was now using them as containers for displaying wares, such as packaged tea, coffee, and a few other small craft items I was selling on commission for the local people.

After scanning the store, he glanced outside, grinning at the antique gas pump, which Chet had rejuvenated.

"Did you know that Missouri has more dying towns than any other state?" he asked. I was expecting him to say something complimentary about the store since he was studying it with approval printed all over his face.

"No," I said, startled at his comment.

"It does." He leaned over to grab a package of cookies on the bakery counter. "And do you know why?"

"I haven't a clue."

"Everywhere else all the little towns have already died. But we in Missouri are too hard-headed and stubborn to let our towns die. They aren't dead, just still dying. We hang on to them. We value their contribution and the rural atmosphere they represent too much. So we buck the national trend and refuse to let them die. We breathe in just enough to keep them alive. Like what you're doing here at Merryman's Crossing.''

He finished his drink and unwrapped his oatmeal cookies. ''This used to be a thriving village—a couple of stores, school, church, blacksmith, grist mill, and several houses. Before US 66 was built, this was the main road to Springfield. The natural ford here made this a major crossing on the river. No other crossing for miles in either direction.''

''Why did that change?''

''The highway bypassed us, cut through half a mile west. But we could still get onto the highway easily. But when it became Interstate 44 with limited access, we were cut off. We used to have to drive several miles on the outer road to get on the interstate until they built the ramp for Highway M last year.''

''So Merryman's Crossing got left by the wayside?''

''Stranded is more like it. Almost killed it outright. There's only this one store that Olen and Faith hung on to and, of course, the post office.'' He paused to take a bite of the cookie. ''Olen and I both fought like tigers to keep the post office when the government tried to close it.''

''I'm surprised they still allow such a small one to continue.''

''We convinced them that there would be enough business to offset the cost of keeping it open. We're almost twenty miles from any other post office. There's lots of local business, mailing, and buying stamps. We're sort of in the category of the post office branches they have in stores like Wal-Mart and in supermarkets.''

I smiled at the picture of our little store compared to a supercenter.

He wadded up the plastic wrapping from his cookie and tossed it expertly into the trash can. ''After Faith's and Olen's deaths, the whole neighborhood worried that you'd close the store. We sort of put on a campaign to persuade you.''

''I noticed. It was pretty obvious, but everyone really helped me that first trial week.''

''Yes, we did.'' He tilted his eyebrow as he smiled. ''And it worked.''

''Yes, it worked. Not so much what they said and did, but because my grandparents had planned it so well. I couldn't let them down.''

''That's what we thought. You see, we weren't going to let this town die. Your grandparents believed that you could put life back into Merryman's Crossing. And you have. That's why they gave the town to you.''

''Gave me a town! I never heard of anyone owning a whole town!''

''Well, it's a very small town. More accurately a hamlet.''

''And one that is dying?''

''Yes.'' He grinned. ''It's been gasping for years but won't give in.''

I laughed at the picture of me giving mouth-to-mouth resuscitation to the big white store building.

Lowell's glance returned to the antique gas pump. "Sold any gas out of the old pump?" I should get used to his abruptly changing the subject.

"Yes, I have. Mostly to people coming in off the interstate. So far nobody has questioned the two cents more per gallon. It's the extra cost of doing it yourself the old-fashioned way that grabs them."

"Reverse psychology?"

"Yeah. Instead of the savings of using self-service pumps, they pay more for the privilege of physically pumping the gas out of the reservoir, watching it fill the glass bubble, and then using the old hose and nozzle to fill their gas tank themselves. You ought to see the expressions on the faces of the people when they do it."

Lowell studied me a few seconds. "You're really something, you know that?"

Though pleased with the compliment, I didn't know how to answer him.

"I bet men are the most interested in the gas pump, aren't they?" he said watching me closely.

"Yes, especially if they have children with them."

"Pay for the privilege of waiting on yourself! Great idea." He shook his head in amazement.

"It wasn't all my idea." I had to be truthful because it never occurred to me that the old pump would still work. "Chet suggested it."

"But not the pay-extra part, I bet."

"No. I thought of that."

"You seem open to all kinds of suggestions. That's a good quality. Most people coming down here from a big city would make this place a carbon copy of city stores."

"That'd be a shame. There is so much charm here."

"Yeah, there is."

"Not being like other stores is the key, I think."

"And because of that and because of you, Merryman's Crossing is still on the dying list, not the dead list of towns."

Lowell had completely shed his county commissioner bearing. Smiling and chatting with me, taking his eyes from me only briefly to glance at changes in the store we were talking about, he was a different guy. Charming, understanding, smart. And so attentive to me that I forgot what he did to Dwight. I didn't want him to leave.

"I've got another thought about the place," I said. He raised his eyebrows in a question. "I wondered about opening up the blacksmith shop across the street and getting Chet to operate it." Since no one else was in the store, and with Lowell's obvious interest and our conversation about dying towns, it seemed like a good time to inspect the old building. And, I must admit, examining it would hold him longer.

"What a great idea! What does he think about that?"

"I haven't asked him. I want to think about it more. Let's go over and see what's there." I started for the door, and then paused, thinking I was too forward. "That is if you've got the time."

"Sure." He stood up, almost knocking down the chair as he swung his leg over it, and hurried to reach my side.

We were at the door when he pulled back. "Oh, wait, I forgot to pay for the cookies. I sure wouldn't want to be accused of stealing." He pulled out some change and tossed it on the counter.

"Don't worry about it," I said. "I'm sure no one would ever accuse you of doing such a thing on purpose." I couldn't help adding, "Sometimes other influences or just not thinking cause us to do things we know aren't right."

Lowell's expression changed slightly. He got my reference to my brother, but he didn't say anything. We walked across the empty road.

"Oh, I haven't got a key." I stopped to return for a hammer. "We'll have to pry loose one of those boards on a window and crawl in."

Laughing at my ignorance, he touched my arm to stop me. "The door never had a lock that I know of." He tramped down the weeds by the double doors, grabbed the latch, and rammed his shoulder against the wood. The door opened inward with creaks and a shower of dust. In the light from the opened doors and what filtered through the spaces between the boards over the windows, we saw one large, very disordered and dusty room.

On the left was a red brick chimney built with an

open forge jutting out from its side. An anvil, set on a rotting cross-section of a log, was nearby. The walls, blackened from smoke, were lined with shelves of handmade tools, hammers, tongs, punches, chisels, and others I didn't recognize. We could hardly find a place to step on the floor for the clutter of trash—iron scraps of all shapes and sizes, and wooden and metal barrels rimmed with rusty horseshoes.

"It's all here!" I exclaimed. I ran around picking up tools, hardly noticing the general disrepair, layers of dust, and abandoned condition.

Lowell was also studying everything. "It's been a long time since I've looked in here. It's been shut up for years."

"I can't imagine that someone hasn't stolen these tools or vandalized the place."

"We don't have much of that here," Lowell said, tensing up. His jovial mood became serious.

I remembered that Dwight said that preventing crime in the county was the platform that got Lowell elected. Since I'd already alluded to Dwight's troubles, to keep Lowell in his pleasant, unofficial mood, I left that subject to marvel over the array of cross-peen hammers laying on a dirty shelf. "It wouldn't take much to get this shop working again." In my enthusiasm I grabbed his hand to pull him with me. "Just look at them."

Instead of looking at the tools, we looked into each other's eyes. When I grabbed his hand, a strange feeling coursed through me. From the expression in his eyes, he must have felt it, too. Instead of removing his hand, he grasped mine tighter.

I was uncomfortable, or maybe embarrassed is the better word. Instead of savoring the moment, or letting Lowell take the next step, I pulled away. To cover my retreat, I skipped down a cleared space, jabbering rapidly, "This place is great. I could do a lot with this. If Chet is willing . . . Do you think he'd be interested?" I didn't look at him to see his answer or give him time to respond. "I bet he would. He spends most mornings on the store porch. And having a blacksmith will help the store. It'll draw people here."

I looked out the cobwebby window toward the low-water bridge. The recent rains kept the river running just over the concrete curbings. If I didn't know the bridge was there, or see the road leading down to the river from both sides, I wouldn't have noticed it. So much water was unusual during the summer months.

I forced my thoughts from my attraction to Lowell back to the problems of increasing business at the store. The bridge was the key. To distance myself from Lowell, I concentrated on the bridge.

All during the past month, the lack of a dependable bridge had been on my mind. While the rains continued and the river ran over the bridge, the salesmen and delivery men complained about being forced to drive through the water. The young mother, Maria, said that the school bus often didn't come after the children up our road. The mail carrier, who left and collected the post office's mail at the store, groaned about it, threatening to complain to the officials and recommend closing the post office. He said, "Your patrons can set a line of boxes out on Highway M and come across the bridge to get their mail. Then when the river is high, it would be their problem, not mine."

During the second week, when the water was several inches deep over the bridge, very few people from the interstate braved the crossing to drive to the store. When the river lowered, so that the six-inch-high concrete sidings were visible to mark the borders of the bridge, some customers ventured over it.

With ideas flitting through my head for the store and a working blacksmith shop, I forgot Lowell's strong reaction earlier when I had suggested a new bridge. "Now," I said, "all we'd need to make Merryman's Crossing a real town again is to get a better bridge."

"Absolutely not!" he blurted out. He retreated a few steps from me, his smile erased.

Another sensitive subject with him. He was a stubborn man, hung up on some silly notions. I retorted, almost angrily, "You just said that Merryman's Crossing was dying. Without a decent bridge, it will surely die. Not a blacksmith shop or anything I do to build up trade at the store will help if people are afraid to cross the river."

Lowell pressed his lips together. His eyebrows lowered into a frown. He wouldn't admit that I was right, though perceptive as he was, he must have realized what a good bridge could do.

I controlled my angry tone. Honey catches more flies than vinegar, as Grandma used to say. "Why are you so against a new bridge?" I asked pleasantly.

"Two reasons. First, the county hasn't the funds." He started out angrily, speaking to me as if I were a moron, but, like me, he controlled his anger. "There are other bridges and roads that take priority. This one serves only the store and the half dozen families that live up the river road here."

I nodded that this reasoning did make sense. "But if the store really takes off, won't people insist that the county fix the bridge?"

He didn't answer or look at me.

"In other places, like Branson," I said, trying to reason with him, "when tourists started coming in droves, roads were built to handle the traffic."

Lowell grunted. "This little crossroads store doesn't compare to Branson."

"No, but that doesn't mean the people up here don't need a way in. They were here before the highway isolated them. The county owes them access." When Lowell didn't respond, I said, "You said one reason was lack of funds. What other reason?"

He was quick to answer. "A high-water bridge would invite all kinds of traffic to come up our way. Now no one but those of us living on the road venture farther than the store. Fix up the bridge and I'll guarantee the world will swarm over us. Vandals, robbers, kids cruising and up to no good, and the like. That'll change the whole aspect of the neighborhood." He spread out his hands in a futile attempt to illustrate the magnitude of the destruction that would occur. His manner didn't suggest that he connected one of those "up-to-no-good kids" to my brother.

Me and my big mouth. I wished I hadn't mentioned the bridge. The pleasant tone of our conversation was ruined. Whatever drew us together there in the old blacksmith shop evaporated. He stood apart from me, half turned away. I didn't say more, but determined from then on to avoid two topics with him—the bridge and my brother.

The next day when Lowell stopped by, he was again in a genial mood, not in any hurry to leave. Neither of us mentioned the bridge. We discussed several ideas I had about the store. The conversation soon centered on the schoolhouse. Since my grandparents' will indicated that Lowell take charge of the music parties that were held in the schoolhouse, I gave him free sway to do whatever he wanted, and to make any needed changes. He agreed to be an unpaid general manager, using the school for a music and community center. That also included using the building for other things, like Merl's and Vivian's wedding. Lowell was willing to take that responsibility from me. Operating the store and finding time to write were all I could manage.

We worked out an agreement. At his discretion, he could collect rent from outside groups to help offset the utility bills. Using some of the funds set aside for me to make changes, I authorized him to carry out the improvements he suggested, like buying a better piano and improving the sound system.

I brought him up to date about the blacksmith shop. Chet was excited about opening it up. I offered him basically the same arrangements as Lowell had for the schoolhouse. I'd finance the improvements if he maintained the building and was in the shop a few days a week. He could sell anything he made, take on custom work, and use the shop for whatever he wanted. I, for my part, would get more customers at the store, as well as the building put back in working order.

Interrupting the discussion of the renovation of the blacksmith shop, Lowell asked, "Do you like to fish?"

Lowell and his change of subjects.

"Uh, I don't really know. I've never done much."

"Want to go fishing Sunday afternoon?" he asked. "I'll show you."

Before I realized he was asking me for a date, I said, "I do my writing then. I need to get started on another chapter."

"Shannon said that you were writing about the fur traders who operated in this area before the Americans came."

"Yes, that's right." I was surprised that Shannon discussed my writing with him.

"Well, what do you know about trapping on these rivers?"

"I've done a lot of research on it. That is what I

was doing in St. Louis when my grandparents died. Why my family couldn't contact me.''

''Not the same. That's just facts and figures. You need to feel the temperature of the water, smell the mud banks full of rotting leaves, and hear the wind whistle through the holes in the bluffs. If you come with me Sunday, I'll show you. You can take notes out in the field, not just from books. I'll bring along some traps, and even though it's not trapping season, I'll show you how to operate them and where to set them.''

''Really?'' I *was* having trouble getting into my story. Being constantly interrupted in the store was one reason. But Lowell probably hit on the main one. I didn't have a good feel for what I was writing. ''Do you know how to trap? Do people still do it?'' I asked.

''Yes to both questions. I've done some, and yeah, there is still a market for pelts.'' When I hesitated about whether to go, he said, ''Sunday's float will be more research on your book. You'll get ideas when you are actually out there on the river. You'll still have to imagine that it's cold instead of this hot July, because trapping is done in the fall and winter when the pelts are at their best.''

''Okay,'' I said, almost in the same tone I had used when I said okay to staying and running the store. But this agreement carried no tremendous obligation or fear that I couldn't live up to my family's faith in me. This time I was elated—research on my book and a whole afternoon with Lowell.

"Good." He smiled. "I'll pick you up at twelve thirty. We'll put in up where old 66 crosses the river and from there float down to the bridge."

I could hardly wait until Sunday.

Chapter Five

Lowell was a different man on the river. In tan cut-offs and brown T-shirt, he was like a boy showing off his skill and knowledge. Expertly, he maneuvered the johnboat up inlets and beside the earthen banks or graveled bars to show me good locations to find tracks of fur-bearing animals. He described beaver, muskrats, raccoons, and otters, their habits, and where and how to set traps.

Much of what he said I already knew from my research, but I didn't tell him so. I loved listening to his deep, melodious voice as I scribbled down notes as rapidly as I could. I missed my laptop but had decided it was too risky to take it in the johnboat, though he assured me that the flat-bottomed boat would not tip over. It was designed for fishing and trapping the Ozark rivers. On my tablet, I wrote as fast as I could.

73

What I didn't know from my research was the personal touch he added to the topic, his experiences, and what it was like to be out on the river.

While he talked and demonstrated by setting some of his traps, placing them in strategic places, and camouflaging them, my imagination clothed him in buckskins. I visualized him with a long beard and greasy hair just like one of my characters, a French mountain man whom my young Osage protagonist befriends. My plot revolved around the adventures of those two characters.

"Now you'll have to imagine it's November or December," Lowell said, wiping the perspiration from his face and replacing his hat. "There would be no leaves on the trees and perhaps a skim of ice along the banks. It'd be quieter, no birds or frogs. Just the ripple of the water over the riffles or slapping against the side of the boat."

Instead of writing down the facts about beavers or the descriptions of the various steel traps used, I wrote down how naturally Lowell's body moved as he scaled the river bank or jumped out of the boat on a gravel bar. I noted the tilt of his head as he searched the bank for a beaver slide, the "aha" expression in his eyes when he located a likely looking place to set a trap.

Lowell struck the side of our aluminum boat with his wooden paddle. "No sounds like this. Of course, your character would have a wooden boat, so even the sound of striking rocks or sliding over the gravel bar would be muted compared to this metallic sound."

He banged on the side of the boat again. "It was still and quiet compared to the continual bombardment of noise today." He tilted his head to listen to the never-ending drone of traffic on the interstate. "In those days there would be just natural noises, the slap of the water, the breeze through the trees. No traffic, no airplanes, and no heavy machinery sounds from the farms or woods." He shook his head slightly in awe. "Can you imagine how it must have been? How minuscule you would feel in all this wilderness, and yet the power you'd feel in being the first to control it?

"That must have been something!"

"What a feeling to be the first trapper to float this river? No one else around to mess up things." He gazed on down the river that was pulling us with it. "Completely self-sufficient, in your own boat loaded with pelts worth hundreds of dollars, letting the river take you to St. Louis. No bosses, no harassment, no one but you and the friendly Osages in this magnificent country." His dark eyes danced, and his eyebrow raised as he smiled. "Wouldn't it be great?"

"Yes, it would."

Right there before my eyes, a major character in my novel that I was having trouble connecting with came to life. True, the Frenchman of the early eighteenth century was a foot shorter than six-foot-two, clean-shaven Lowell, but his coloring matched theirs. His enthusiasm certainly fit, and his ease in handling the boat was perfect for the role. While I was watching Lowell demonstrate trapping the river, the character of my Frenchman began to form. His dedication to his trade and eventual partnership with the young Osage protagonist became real in my mind. I was already inside the head of the Osage boy. I'd given him a name, Dancing Star, and knew how he would take me through the story. But before now, I couldn't get a handle on the mountain man. Watching Lowell let me flesh out the fictional man, his traits and demeanor.

I was beginning to understand the modern man before me. His tough policy on juvenile crime and his objection to improving the river crossing were attempts to retain the frontier past.

"Back then," Lowell said, "the river was crystal clear, even when it was up, not murky like it is now. With the land all forested, there was less run-off, so the river level didn't fluctuate as much as now. No gravel bars, either, or very few. The eddies were deeper."

He held his paddle behind him in the water, like a rudder, guiding the boat while the current took us down a long eddy. "I've been doing all the talking," he said after a long pause while I caught up on my notes. "Tell me more about your novel."

He wasn't merely being polite. He listened attentively, nodding at parts that I thought were going well and puckering his eyebrows in thought during spots he didn't understand. I explained my revised story line that incorporated my new insight into my secondary character. Though I rarely discussed my writing with anyone before I had the draft completely written, I explained the problem I was having with the beginning of the third chapter. I hadn't figured out how to logically get into the action. When I finished outlining the basic plot of the novel, we brainstormed until I knew just how to write it.

Though I was greatly enjoying the outing and being with Lowell, I was also anxious to get back to my computer to write while my thoughts were fresh and still full of the river. If I had my computer and no interruptions, I believed I could have written the whole book right there. It was in my mind just ready to spill out.

All the information Lowell was giving me, my own research, my ideas, and my background were up there somewhere just swirling around. Until now they had been whirling so that I couldn't make sense of them. The day on the river with Lowell fit the pieces together into a new awareness that gave direction and meaning to my storyline.

I was sitting on the edge of my seat in the front of the boat. During the float I had faced forward, twisting around frequently to watch Lowell. Now I swivelled completely around, facing upriver where we had just been. Lowell, confident, smiling his eyebrow-lifting grin, completely at ease with himself and his surroundings, was framed on either side by the river and its banks of varied-green foliage. The sun burning down from the sky capped the picture.

I was too excited to sit still and too keyed up to take more notes, even though Lowell kept adding information and suggesting other ideas to use in my story. I wanted to get home to write; I wanted the float trip to go on forever. I wanted him to stop exciting me so; I wanted him to continue talking to me. And never to stop looking at me with those intense eyes!

Before I inherited the store, no matter what else I was doing or what experiences I was having, my writing took priority. If my temporary job was too demanding, I resigned. When friends monopolized my time, I made excuses and went home to write. When I was deep into a story, I'd skip meals and go without sleep to get the words down. I lived in my characters. Their adventures were mine. They were my life.

Because of the store this past month, I hadn't been able to operate in my usual way. The store took most of my time, yet I couldn't resign. At the expense of sleep, I did manage to squeeze in time to write at night or early in the morning. Before, when I was on a roll, the words and ideas that congregated in my mind demanded I stop whatever I was doing and put them down on paper or into my computer. I would write happily for hours. But my mounting excitement as we floated down the river was not elation about working out a writing problem, although I had. Normally this breakthrough created excitement and satisfaction enough for me. But on the float trip, the excitement I experienced was more than I'd ever known from writing. Much more. It was Lowell.

He was holding the paddle in the water behind him, occasionally moving it slightly to keep the long, narrow boat where he wanted it. While talking, he continued to scan our surroundings, the cloudless sky, the heavily wooded banks, and the blue heron that kept landing just ahead of us as we floated lazily down toward the bridge at Merryman's Crossing. His gaze returned to me at every sweep of the banks or view of the sky. I could feel it burning into me when I wasn't looking at him, or I'd catch him studying me when our eyes met.

Though I was anxious to get to my computer to write while I was fresh with ideas, stronger than that was my wish for the afternoon to go on forever. Much too soon, I saw that we were already near the store. In dismay I caught a glimpse of the big white building through the trees; the bridge, and the end of the float, were just around the bend.

Lowell's head jerked toward the left bank. He pointed to a narrow, matted-down animal path in the reeds along a muddy bank. "Look," he exclaimed, "a beaver slide!" Immediately our conversation jumped from my plotting to trapping. He back-paddled to keep the boat beside the slide. Even I could see from the dampness and clear paw prints that beavers had used the slide recently. I grabbed an overhanging sycamore limb to hold us in place as he picked up a number forty-four, long-spring trap from the bottom of the boat and set the trigger with a tight tension. He explained that was so only a large beaver would spring it.

He described in detail how to set traps for beaver.

"Finding the beaver's den is best," he said, "but a slide is good." He was the excited boy again. "See right here, trappers would place a couple of traps about eighteen inches apart, the length of a beaver's leg spread. They put the traps about twelve inches deep to catch the back foot. That is . . ." He looked up at me and at my idle pen with an expression that asked why I wasn't writing this down. Jolted back to the purpose of our float trip, I reddened because I was admiring how deftly his strong hands handled the round steel trap. I hastily scribbled down what he had said.

He continued, "Now it's better to catch a beaver in the hind foot because . . ." He stopped for a few seconds, looked down the river with a quizzical expression, and then asked, "What's going on?" The tone of his voice had changed.

Concentrating on my notes, I didn't know what he meant. I looked up at him. His festive manner had changed; his body tensed up. Sitting rigidly upright, with his county commissioner expression back on his face, he frowned as he looked over my head down the river.

"Some more of those young punks!" he said in anger.

I heard a car motor rev up and then stop. Then there were excited voices, a child's and both a man's and a woman's. I turned around to see what he was looking at.

Lowell made a series of powerful strokes with his

paddle. We rounded the bend to see a blue van stalled in the middle of the river. Of course, the van was on the bridge, but from our angle and with the river flowing over the bridge, the van appeared like a boat on top of the water, its wheels sunk down a few inches. In the driver's seat an agitated man was trying to restart the engine. The woman was standing in the water, grasping the opened back door behind the driver. She was crying out, not screaming, but giving low moaning sounds. From the back of the van came the voices of terrified children. A little girl's frightened face was pressed against the front seat window.

When Lowell realized they weren't "punks," his whole demeanor changed. He paddled rapidly toward the bridge, calling out in a reassuring voice, "Hold on, lady. Get back in the van. I'll get you out. You're not in any danger. Just get back in the van."

The lady stopped crying but made no move to get back into the van. As we drew closer, I saw that she was having trouble standing up. The current, swirling past the van's wheels, was sucking her feet toward the low concrete rims marking the sides of the bridge. But those rims, plus her firm grasp on the van's door, were what kept her from being washed over the side.

"I can't get back," the woman cried.

"Just stay there. Hold on," Lowell shouted as we drew nearer. "I'll help you." And to allay any fears they might have about us, he added, "I'm Lowell Boyd, and this is Kay Merryman. We live up the road."

The man in the van said, "I started to back up when I saw how strong the current was, but I killed the engine. I can't get it started again."

"Hold on," Lowell repeated. By now we had reached the bridge. Lowell beached the boat in a washed-out place right by the bridge on the bank opposite the store. I jumped out and pulled the prow out of the water.

"Don't worry," he called to the driver. "The bridge is safe. I'll get you across." He climbed out of the boat, tied it to a tree, and without looking back to see what I'd do, he hurried to the road. Not pausing to test the strength of the current, he waded out onto the bridge. I was just a few footsteps behind him. When he realized I was with him, he waded around the van to the driver and motioned me go behind the van to reach the woman.

Holding on to the door post with one hand, because the current was sucking my feet out, threatening to wash me over the side, I used my other hand to steady the woman. With the door on one side and me on the other, the woman turned around slowly and climbed back into the backseat of the van beside two small boys. They threw their arms about her. Then, holding on to the van, I waded around it to the other side where there was more room and less danger of the rush of water pushing me off the bridge.

The current was strong, but not dangerously so. When I was a kid, I used to run across the bridge many times when the river was over it like now. I knew to keep to the upriver side of the bridge so that the force of the current wouldn't wash me overboard. And though the river was murky, I could see the concrete side rims.

While I calmed the woman and children, Lowell and the driver managed to start the engine. Guided by Lowell, who waded shin deep through the water ahead of the van to mark the middle of the bridge, the man drove on across the bridge.

"We were just driving around," he explained when we were all safely off the bridge on the gravel road. "I'd heard of Merryman's Crossing and decided to see it."

"I told him not to cross," the woman said. "But he wouldn't listen."

"And I told you not to get out," the man retorted.

"If we were going to drown, I didn't want us trapped in the van," she said. Then addressing Lowell, she asked, "Now how do we get back on the highway? We're on the wrong side of the river. And we'll not drive across that again." She looked back at the bridge and shuddered.

"It's really not dangerous if you don't back up," Lowell said. "Your husband just got nervous is all and killed his engine."

"When I got onto the bridge, I could feel the force of the water push the van to one side," the man said. "I was afraid to go all the way across for fear I couldn't get back. So since we'd come just a little ways, I thought backing up would be the best way. But my rear wheels hit the curbing and I . . .''

"Don't worry about it," Lowell said. "People make the crossing through the water all the time. It's not dangerous."

The man looked back at the bridge that was almost hidden by the water rushing across it and shook his head. He plainly did not agree.

"It'll be okay. Just drive up that little rise there to the store where there's room to turn around," Lowell said pointing out the building. "We'll wait here to see you safely back over."

The children in the van were no longer scared, only excited at the adventure. They waved to us as the van crept up the hill to the store.

"Crazy guy," Lowell said to me, "trying to back up. He wasn't in any danger, but he'd have surely driven off if he'd gone any farther. Good thing he killed his engine."

I started to say something like, "See what I mean about the bridge?" but I stopped myself in time. The day had been too pleasant to ruin it with talk about the bridge, which would surely bring on his bad mood.

On his way back, the driver paused by us before he tackled the bridge. "Thanks, Mr. Boyd."

Lowell nodded. "Just go slowly. You can see the sides of the bridge. Stay in the middle. And don't stop."

"I won't," he said. The woman behind him had a firm grasp on the back of her husband's seat as if that would protect them all. The children looked expectantly out of the windows, calmed by Lowell's presence and promise that the river wouldn't hurt them. "Say," the man continued, "aren't you a county official of some kind? Your name sounds familiar."

"Yeah, I'm county commissioner."

The man looked at Lowell and shook his head. "Ought to have a decent bridge here. This one is an accident waiting to happen. As county commissioner you should know that and do something about it." He let his van coast to the bridge. When his wheels hit the water, he inched across, barely disturbing the currents in the river. When safely on the other side, he honked his horn and waved his hand out the window. Then he sped up across the flat land and disappeared around the bend that went up the hill to Highway M. Dust whirled around in the heat.

Lowell was no longer the happy boy on the river. "C'mon, Kay," he said, struggling with his commissioner persona, "let's get the boat and call it a day."

He grabbed my hand. Side by side, we waded back across the bridge to the boat. The water running over our canvas shoes was cool in the ninety-degree heat. Lowell paddled us back across the river, and while I unloaded the boat and carried the gear to the road, he went to the store to get his pickup. Without speaking more than was necessary, we loaded the johnboat and gear into the back of his pickup.

"I had a great day," I said when he stopped at the

store to let me out. "You were right. Now I know what it was really like to trap on these rivers."

"I'm glad. I enjoyed it. Too bad about those people on the bridge ruining it." He wiped the perspiration from his face and put his wide-brimmed hat back on his head.

"They didn't ruin it. Just showed another side of you—a knight in shining armor going to the rescue of a damsel in distress."

He pulled his T-shirt out from his chest and slapped his bare legs. "Shining armor, eh?"

"Well, you did help a lady in distress."

"As I recall, Kay, you were the one who waded in to rescue her."

"Okay, okay. But you got the van out of danger."

Our bantering back and forth put a smile back on his face.

"Don't forget the music party Saturday night," he said just before he drove off.

"Oh, yeah. Anything I can do to help?"

"I'll let you know." His pickup wheels spun as he sped up the road, a cloud of dust following him.

Chapter Six

I heard the guitars and fiddles tuning up in the schoolhouse across the lawn while there were still customers in the store. I intended to close up early to help Lowell and Shannon get ready before people arrived, but a busload of tourists headed to Branson pulled up just as I was locking the door. A young woman, dressed in navy slacks and light blue blouse with an insignia above the pocket, jumped out of the bus. She looked around in amazement before spotting me on the porch. Men and women were looking out of the windows, pointing and talking with one another.

"Can I help you?" I figured they had missed their turn and wanted directions.

"We're looking for Merryman's Crossing Store," the woman said. "And from your sign this must be the place." She sort of shook her head at the faded, almost unreadable sign. With so much to do, I hadn't repainted it yet.

"Yes. This is it."

"Good," she said happily and popped back into the bus. I heard her say, "Okay, folks. We'll stop here for thirty minutes." About two dozen couples and a few single women filed out of the bus. Most of the people, amazed at the store's old-fashioned look, immediately walked up on the porch. Three couples headed across the road to the blacksmith shop where Chet, in his faded blue overalls and greasy cap, was still working at his forge

"How'd you find us?" I asked the tour guide while unlocking the door and stepping back to let the customers in. "We've never had a bus come here before."

"We keep our ears open for interesting places to stop for a break on our long drive from Chicago. On my last trip, I heard about an authentic country store with an intriguing name. So when the driver saw the highway department sign for gas service at the interstate exit with your store the only gas station listed, we all wanted to check you out." She took in the store, the schoolhouse, the blacksmith shop, the country road, the river curling around my acres of hills, bluffs, and open meadows. Even the mysterious stream of mist on the hill was showing right on cue, like Old Faithful. "Wow! It's even better than I heard. You've got a perfect jewel here. Don't change a thing."

"I wasn't too sure about that bridge back there," the bus driver said, coming behind us. "I stopped on the other side, about to turn around when a couple of cars came by. They said the school bus goes over it all the time, so I figured it would be okay to cross."

"Yes, it's structurally sound." I didn't say anything about usually having to drive through water, because during the past week since our float trip, with no additional rain, the river level had fallen to barely lapping the floor of the bridge.

I spent a busy and profitable half hour answering the many questions about the history of the store and tallying up purchases. Several of Steve's baskets and Clyde's carvings sold, as well as some of the rag rugs, crocheted items, and other handicraft items I had for sale. Nora's home baking disappeared quickly, along with drinks and other snack foods. I could barely keep up with the demand. I wished Nora was there to answer the questions for me.

I decided after the fifth person asked to use the rest room that a modern public rest room would be my next improvement with my grandparents' money. Instead of sending the customers to the two outhouses behind the schoolhouse, which my regular customers used, I directed them upstairs to the bathroom in my house. No matter how thrilled these tourists were with the old-fashioned look, I knew that interest wouldn't include using the two-holers. Maybe I'd build something outside that looked like an outhouse, but had modern stools and basins. I'd think about that.

"Everything is perfect here," one shorts-clad woman said. "except you."

When I stammered some inane response, she laughed and quickly added, "Everything is authentic but you. Your shorts, baggy T-shirt, and short hairdo just don't fit."

"That's right," her husband said, "you ought to have a long braid under a sunbonnet and wear a feed sack apron over a long calico dress."

"That'll be the day," I said, shuddering at the thought.

The woman said, "You could dress the part like that colorful blacksmith across the road. He's perfect for the part."

I laughed. "That's the way Chet Hollis dresses most of the time."

"Great place here," the man said as he slapped down his credit card for the items his wife had heaped in one of Steve's baskets.

Before the bus left, most of the tourists had crossed the street to the blacksmith shop. A few wandered up to the schoolhouse to listen to the music and peer inside the one-room country school. Though invited to come in and join the party, the tour guide shook her head. They didn't have time.

"Come back," I said to her as she rounded up her charges and ushered them back into the bus.

"I surely will. Next trip I'll schedule more time. I'll let you know when we come through." She took down my address and phone number.

"Great."

I was elated. I had hoped that more individual tourists would stop by, but I hadn't thought of busloads of people with vacation money burning their wallets. It made perfect sense. A short way from the interstate, the store was just a little over an hour from Branson where hundreds of buses arrived every day, many of them passing by us down I-44.

Chet and I stood in the road watching the bus slowly cross the bridge and pick up speed as it climbed the hill to the highway. He grinned and patted my shoulder.

"Kay, girl, you sure know what you're a-doin' here. I sold ever last one of them nutcrackers I made. They almost took all my horseshoe nail rings, too."

"Did a tour bus ever stop here before?"

"Not that I knowed. Reckon this one's a fluke? Driver got lost or something?"

"No, they came here on purpose. The guide said she'd heard about us."

Chet beamed happily. "Then others will come, too. I better get busy making more stuff. I thought of making little horseshoes with Merryman's Crossing on them. I think small stuff will sell, don't you?" He didn't wait for my response. "Them people sure were excited about findin' us." He emphasized the "us," proud that he was now an official part of the business.

He removed his brown leather cap, ran his hand through his thinning white hair, and mopped the perspiration from his forehead with his red bandana handkerchief. His pale blue eyes looked at me with admiration. "Kay, girl, your grandpa and grandma would sure be proud of you. And they had you pegged right to give this to you. Merryman's Crossing is back on the map." He did a quick jig right there in the road, grabbing me and swinging me around, ending with a do-si-do. I don't ever remember being this thrilled, unless it was when I sold my first book.

When I locked up the store again and hurried to the schoolhouse, the music was going strong. Cars and pickups had been arriving while I was busy at the store. As soon as I entered, Nora greeted me. I said, "I sure needed you to talk to those people. They were full of questions about everything. One lady wanted to know exactly how to make butter in Grandma's old wooden churn. I didn't know. You'll have to show me."

She grinned, pleased that I valued her help. "Next time I see a bus a-comin', I'll come right over and help you." She led me to a desk near the front. We were both small enough to slip in the double seat. "You really need someone else to help you in the store. It takes two people. You can't keep on all by yourself."

"I know. It's demanding too much time. Even Sundays, people come in. I should stay open then."

"Good idea. Sh-h. Lowell is just about to start," Nora said, pointing to the front where he and Shannon were making the final adjustments to the microphone and conferring with the musicians.

The schoolroom looked just as it must have in the 1930s. It was crowded; some people were seated at the old wooden desks and on folding chairs, while others stood up against the walls. A few kids were outside, sitting on the stoop or playing tag around the building. I didn't know half of the people. I wondered how there was an empty seat left for me, then realized that Nora must have saved it for me. I waved to Merl and Vivian across the room and nodded at other neighbors and people I'd met. I saw Maria with her little boy. Nora's comment about needing help gave me an idea. Maybe Maria would work for me instead of having to drive to town and pay for baby-sitting. She could keep her little boy at the store. I figured out what I could afford to pay her. It might just work out.

At the front, on the stagelike platform raised one step above the floor, were six or seven men and women with guitars, fiddles, mandolins, dobros, and a bass. Though they had been playing informally for the past half hour as people gathered, they were now relaxing, waiting for Lowell to begin the official program. In the back, piled on a couple of tables, were boxes and covered baskets of food. There was a tub full of ice with soft drinks and a big water cooler with paper cups beside it. I sighed with pleasure. I could relax. This was Lowell's responsibility. I intended to enjoy the evening.

"Welcome, folks," Lowell said above the din of talking. His deep, strong voice needed no amplification. He stepped off the stage away from the microphone to be closer to the audience. Holding out both hands in a welcome sign, he was completely at ease and handsome in his white Stetson hat and blue jeans. When the noise died down, he said, "We've been jamming up here waiting for the crowd to gather. Now we're about to start in earnest. I've got the names of the regulars who play or sing, but if there are any others, raise your hands and Shannon will put you on the list."

A few people in the audience raised their hands. Shannon went to each. She looked cute in her full western-style skirt, her fitted shirt with embroidered horses across the front, and tooled boots. Her cowboy hat was dangling from its string on her back. She squeezed my hand in welcome as she passed down the aisle by me and whispered, "Is Dwight coming?"

I shrugged my shoulders. I hadn't heard much from him lately since he was working overtime at the boat factory, earning as much as he could to pay off his fine. He continued to mail me notes to give to Shannon when Lowell wasn't around. He didn't address them directly to Shannon for fear that Lowell would beat her to the mail.

Lowell continued, "Each musician or group plays two numbers to start with. When we get through the list and have time, you can play more. Then afterwards, as usual, we'll jam here as long as anyone wants to stay."

He waited while Shannon wrote the new names on the blackboard under the ones already there; people then knew when their turns came. Finished with the list, Shannon turned back to the audience. A big smile spread over her face as she looked over our heads to the door at the back. I followed her gaze. My brother stood in the doorway, grinning back at her. Behind Dwight were my parents. Mom waved to me and indicated they would join Uncle Bruce and Aunt Betsy in the row of folding chairs under the windows on their right.

Lowell's expression changed when he spotted Dwight standing tall and easy near the door; he frowned when he noticed Shannon's reaction to Dwight's presence.

Lowell got everyone's attention again. "Most of you know that Olen and Faith Merryman gave Merryman's Store to their granddaughter, Kay. In the past few weeks she has not only kept the store going, but has added inventory and along with Chet Hollis has opened up the old blacksmith shop." There was some scattered applause.

"Olen and Faith also asked me to take charge of the schoolhouse and the gatherings here. Kay and I have already done some things to make it more comfortable—the new air-conditioning unit in the window, for example." The applause this time was unanimous. Some men whistled as everyone looked at me and back to Lowell.

"We still have lots to do," he continued. "In addition to the music parties, the schoolhouse will be available for private parties. To pay the upkeep expenses, there will be a fee. See me or Kay about that. And for those of you who haven't been here before, we still use the picturesque privies out back.'' While the audience laughed, I realized that my idea of building outside rest rooms would help the schoolhouse as well. I marveled at how everything seemed to come together so well.

"Now, folks, before we begin the program I want to recognize the members of the Merryman family. I think they are all here.'' He introduced Uncle Bruce, Aunt Betsy, and Merl as a group. He made Vivian stand up and get everyone's congratulations on her upcoming marriage into the Merryman family. There was enthusiastic applause for that, with some whistles and comments.

Next he introduced my parents and Dwight. When he said Dwight's name, his voice did not change, but I noticed a tightening of his jaws, and he did not look into Dwight's eyes as he had the other family members'.

"And last,'' he said, his voice back to normal and zeroing in on me, "here's Kay Merryman, our hostess.'' There was a roar of clapping and whistles. I recognized Merl's and Dwight's yahoos. Nora pushed me out of the seat as Lowell came to me and led me up to the platform. He removed the microphone from its stand and thrust it in my hand.

There was dead silence in the room. A sea of faces smiled expectantly at me. I was petrified. I am a writer, not a speaker. When I'm not closeted with my fictional characters, I'm the one over in the corner observing, taking notes, the one encouraging others to talk. The one watching the personal dramas taking place as people interacted. Never the one in the spotlight. Invisible—that's me. That's the way I like it.

When I just stood there, awkward and silent, Lowell must have sensed my fear. He retrieved the mike. "Folks, we won't ask her to say anything this time." Turning to me, he said in his musical voice, "Thank you, Kay, for putting so much life back into Merryman's Crossing."

I started back to my seat, but Lowell held my arm. The men and women on the stage held their instruments ready to play. "Now," Lowell said, nodding to them, "here's our unofficial Merryman's Crossing band to begin the program. Let's make music." Immediately the room was filled with a lively tune that I didn't know. Lowell escorted me back to my seat as people we passed smiled at me.

"That's okay, child," Nora said, patting my hand as I slid into the seat. "Lowell shouldn't have sprung that on you. We all get tongue-tied in front of a mike." I couldn't imagine her ever getting tongue-tied anywhere, but I appreciated her comforting words. Safely in my seat, I thought of several things I could have said. Even "I'm happy to be here and thanks for coming" would have been enough. But like a dummy, I just stood there. Perhaps if Lowell had given me a piece of chalk and led me to the blackboard, I could have written down something I couldn't say. I shook myself. What a silly thought!

The music party was very informal, not like a concert. With Lowell as host, it was like a well-organized family gathering. People milled around, inside and outside, sometimes visiting as one after another, the musicians, singly or in groups, took their turns. Gospel, bluegrass, folk, country, and popular music filled the house and escaped out the doors and poorly fitting windows into the hot night air outside. Some of the musicians were quite good, others not so, but no one cared. Everyone was there to participate, to listen to music, and to visit.

I thought I was there to observe, as usual, but unwittingly, I was forced into the center of attention. At one time or another, everyone came to chat with me, to talk about the store, and tell me stories about Olen and Faith. Nora stuck by me, introducing me to those I did not know, and deftly took over the conversation when I wanted to excuse myself to visit with some of my family.

About halfway through the evening, the women spread out the food. I threaded through the crowd to get a cold drink. I was visiting with Shannon by the water cooler when Dwight appeared between us. We kidded around about me being tongue-tied. While they were chatting, the glances between Shannon and Dwight became intense. They obviously were not listening to me telling about the tourist bus or even explaining the preparations for Merl and Vivian's upcoming wedding.

"This is absurd!" I thought I said this to myself, but when Dwight looked at me in surprise, I realized I'd spoken out loud.

"What is?" he asked.

"You two having to sneak around Lowell."

"Please don't," Shannon said, frowning and cocking her head to indicate her brother coming down the aisle toward us.

Lowell reached Shannon's side and took her hand. If looks could kill, Dwight would be dead from Lowell's threatening glare. "Come with me," he ordered Shannon, pulling her away.

"She doesn't have to," Dwight said, facing him squarely. "She's an adult now and can choose her own friends. She doesn't have to do what you say anymore." I gave Dwight credit; he kept his cool, speaking in a confident voice I'd not heard before.

"I'm telling you for the last time: Stay away from my sister." Lowell's voice was not as controlled as Dwight's. Noticing a few people watching him, he spoke more quietly, yet in the tone of voice he expected people to obey. "You must leave *now*."

I had all I could take. This was my little brother being bullied like when we were kids. No matter that he was now a grown man six inches taller and many pounds heavier than I, old habits don't die easily. No one was going to pick on Dwight while I was around.

I faced Lowell, my mouth held stubbornly firm and

my eyes blazing. "He does not have to leave. This is *my* property and no one can order my brother off. Not even you, Mr. County Commissioner."

Stunned, Lowell stared at me. I saw the anger in his eyes. I didn't care. Let him have some of his own attitude back. Both Shannon and Dwight tried to quiet me. Mom and Dad, seeing the confrontation, started to come over until Dwight waved them back. But none of them could stop what I had to say.

"Dwight is a fine young man who made a stupid mistake. Didn't you ever do anything you regretted? He didn't hurt anyone or anything. He never did anything like that before, and he never will again. He's working long hours of overtime to atone for the mistake, and so he can attend the university next fall. You should be proud of him and encourage him instead of trying to ruin his life."

Lowell continued to stare at me for a few seconds, his expression changing from anger and resentment to hurt because I talked to him like this. Perhaps it hadn't occurred to him before how I'd feel about his involvement in Dwight's trouble. He then glanced back at the people in the room. A few were beginning to notice us. The lively music from the platform and the singer's spirited voice did not match our angry moods.

His mouth was set in a hard line. "Then I guess I'm the one who has to leave," he said so quietly that I had to strain to hear him. Then he strode toward the door.

"No," Shannon, Dwight, and I all said almost together.

"Don't leave," I said to Lowell's back.

"I'll talk to him," Shannon said, putting her hand on my arm to hold me as I started to go after him. I couldn't read from the look she sent Dwight whether she was proud of him or dismayed. She followed Lowell outside.

The performers finished and were gathering up their instruments as the next act on the list, a lone man with a guitar, walked to the front. What to do? Lowell was gone. Someone had to introduce the next number. Not me. No way was I going to stand in front of all these people. Merl! He could take over.

I reached him and Vivian, who were sharing a piece of pecan pie, too absorbed with each other to notice anything else in the room. "Merl," I asked, roughly pulling him to his feet. "Could you take over as emcee? Lowell had to leave."

Merl glanced around the room. Many people were looking at us, wondering why no one was in charge. "Uh? Sure, I guess I can," he said.

Under his leadership the music continued uninterrupted.

"Maybe I ought to leave," Dwight said in my ear over the loud voice of the man singing an old-fashioned hymn into the microphone.

"No. You stay here." I was still angry. "No one but I can say who can and can't be on my property.

Certainly not Lowell, even if Grandpa and Grandma gave him the authority to handle the music parties.''

"But if he quits, then you will have to take charge or the parties will stop.''

Dwight was right. I couldn't have that. I had enough responsibility without adding the schoolhouse, too. The music parties were a long-time tradition. I didn't want that to stop. And now that I'd calmed down some and quit shaking with anger, I remembered how charming Lowell was on the float trip. How the arch of his neck curved into his tan shirt. How my spirits lifted whenever I looked at him.

"I better leave,'' Dwight said again. "I can't ruin everything. I can tell you like him, don't you?'' I didn't answer. "Shannon says he talks about you a lot. Fess up, sister, you like him.''

"Yes, but . . .''

"Then let this go. Shannon will handle him.''

"I thought you hated him. At the lawyer's office you . . .''

"Yes . . . no. Not really. I'm working on that. I sort of see his point. He thinks he's protecting Shannon, like you protect me. She said if we give him time, he'll come around. Don't make it worse for all of us.''

"Okay,'' I said. Now Dwight was the mature one giving me advice.

"Good for you,'' Nora whispered as I slipped into my seat beside her. She had obviously witnessed our confrontation at the refreshment table. "And good for Dwight, too.''

By the time the gospel singer finished his two pieces, Lowell and Shannon had returned. Shannon touched my arm and smiled to let me know it was all right. Lowell walked to the front to let Merl know he was back.

"While I have the floor," Merl said to the audience, "I'd like to invite all of you to Vivian and my wedding Saturday, July twenty-fourth right here in the schoolhouse."

"It's about time you two was gettin' hitched," someone said.

Others agreed.

Merl grabbed Vivian. With his arm around her waist, he said, "Yes, it is. And we want everyone to celebrate with us."

"What time?" someone asked.

"Three o'clock."

"And the reception right after," Vivian said, smiling up at Merl, her dimples showing in both cheeks. The audience clapped.

"I'll come," Lowell said.

"You better, you're going to sing," Vivian said.

"Don't worry. Thanks, Merl, for pinch-hitting for me." He walked to the blackboard and wrote in Merl's and Vivian's name to be the next number. He turned to the audience. "Folks, I think it's fitting that Merl Merryman and Vivian Coffey be next." The audience clapped and whistled.

Nora grinned at me. She then looked at Lowell, who was stepping off the platform when Merl and Vivian began their duet. He stationed himself in the corner across the room from me, not once looking my way. "He'll come around." Nora said the same words that Shannon had used. She tapped my hand that was laying on the initials carved long ago in the old oaken desktop.

Accompanying them first on his guitar, then switching to a fiddle and mandolin, Merl sang in perfect harmony to Vivian's soprano as the two sang to each other as if no one was within a hundred miles of them. If any two people belonged together it was these two. And about time.

I sent a silent thanks to my grandparents, whose bequest was making it happen.

Chapter Seven

Lowell didn't stop by the store on his way to town on Monday or Tuesday as he usually did. Instead, right on schedule, his pickup speeded by the store, not even slowing for the slope down to the river or when he drove across the bridge.

Tuesday, Shannon rode in just behind him on her mare. Jumping off and tying her mount to the hitching post, which was still there from horse-and-buggy days, she entered the store, letting the door slam behind her. When she saw me looking out the window at the dust Lowell's truck left behind, she said, "He's stubborn, but manageable. You have to be patient."

"I don't see why he's mad at me. He started it." Even as I said it, I realized I sounded like a pouty kid.

Shannon laughed. "No, actually Dwight started it with that juvenile stunt with the motorcycle. No way could Lowell excuse that. Then I made him mad at the music party when I purposely went to Dwight right in his face. I knew it would upset Lowell, but I hadn't seen Dwight for so long. He looked so handsome and so . . . I don't know what. So manly. So grown up. I just had to talk to him.''

Nodding my understanding, I said, ''Then I got mad when Lowell ordered Dwight out of the schoolhouse, like my brother was trash or something. Lowell had no right whatsoever to do that. I couldn't help telling him off.''

Shannon giggled. ''Pretty silly, isn't it?''

I agreed.

''Now Lowell is mad at all of us and we're all mad at him,'' she said.

''So what do we do?'' I asked.

''Nothing.''

''We can't do nothing. This can't go on. We all need to work together here at Merryman's Crossing. Dwight will come to the store often. When he starts college he may stay with me some so he doesn't have to drive so far. Besides that, you kids have a right to see each other if you want.''

''You're just like Dwight,'' Shannon said in an adult tone as if she were explaining life to a child. ''You're too impatient. Though Lowell can't see it, he *is* the problem. He can't get beyond what Dwight did. He won't see him as he really is. So, just cool it for a while. I know how to handle my brother. He's already coming around. What you said to him the other night about Dwight working overtime and going to the university, that impressed Lowell. If we handle him right, by the end of summer he won't object any more.''

"I'm not so sure about Dwight,'' I said. "He's really mad at your brother, and I don't blame him. Lowell was extra hard on him and went out of his way to use his influence in a matter that wasn't in his department. From what I understand, the motorcycle wasn't damaged at all. A misdemeanor at most.''

"No, the bike wasn't hurt. The guys just cruised around on it. Dwight's paying for the bike wasn't what Lowell wanted. This incident was a chance for him to show the county that he was going to wipe out crime. Make the criminals pay. Justice, and all that. Dwight's timing was all wrong!''

"Lowell didn't have to come down so hard.''

"No, he didn't. But you've got to know where he's coming from. I sometimes think he's in the wrong century. He believes he can return us to some ideal pioneer time when he imagines people were more honest and more neighborly. Not as much crime and stuff like that. He's trying to bring that back.''

"But instead he's making us all suffer.''

"Yes.'' Shannon sighed. Though she was the younger sister in her family, I realized what a burden Shannon carried. She was looking after her brother, while he thought *he* was the strong one.

Some tourists came into the store, and Shannon picked up her groceries. When she paid me, she said,

"Just be cool. Can't risk ruining everything. And not just Dwight and my chances." She grinned at me. "There's you and the Honorable Mr. Stubbornpuss."

"We're not . . ."

"I know, you're just friends. That's what Lowell says, but he brings you into every conversation we've had since you've come back. Don't ruin it." She ran out the door, vaulted on her mare, and galloped up the road to her ranch.

Just as Shannon predicted, the next day Lowell stopped to fill his gas tank and for his customary Nora cinnamon roll, a carton of orange juice, and a cup of coffee.

"That was a good music party the other night," I said as he pulled some bills from his wallet. I couldn't tell from his attitude whether he planned to talk a bit as he had been doing, or revert back to his earlier pop-in run-out appearances. "Everyone really enjoyed it."

"Yeah, they did, didn't they? Especially the air-conditioning." Our laughter eased the tension.

"And at the end when Chet bragged about the tour bus buying him out and doing that hoedown. That brought the house down."

"Yes, it was a good party." Lowell didn't look at me, though I was studying him to gauge his mood. He didn't say anything as he carefully put his bills in his wallet, the ones together and the five behind them. He didn't seem in a hurry to leave.

To fill the long pause, I said, "I was disappointed that you didn't do a number."

"Not enough time. It was getting late, and I wanted to make sure everyone else got a chance to perform. I'll do one or two next time."

Though we were acting as if our heated exchange of words on Saturday night had never happened, that confrontation hung in the air between us.

After another long pause, he asked, "How're you coming along with your novel?"

That was a safe subject. And one I wanted to talk about. I babbled on about how I had completely revised the first few chapters and was well into another. I started giving more details about what I'd done to the story before I realized that he was only half listening. My novel wasn't the topic he wanted to talk about.

In midsentence about Dancing Star's good catch of beaver, I blurted out, surprising even myself, "I'm sorry about my outburst the other night."

Lowell's expression revealed that was the subject on his mind. "No," he said, cupping my hand that lay on the counter, "No, I was the one that was out of line."

"We both overreacted. Let's forget it."

He nodded, his tight lips relaxing at the corners. He squeezed my hand and turned to leave.

I can't believe even yet what I did next or where the idea came from. I was acting like my characters did, taking charge of the situation and making things happen. "Would you like to walk with me up on the bluff and around my property? I don't even know exactly what all I have here, except lots of trees and rocks.''

He was startled at my question. Afraid that he would refuse and to cover my embarrassment, I rattled on. ''I've been so busy I haven't even done my usual jogging or walking. There's an intriguing mist I sometimes see over there.'' I waved my hand toward the back of the store, indicating the forested land behind the building. ''I thought that you might show me around and . . .''

''Whoa, Kay. Slow down. Of course, I'll walk with you. What about this Sunday?''

''Great.'' My heart leaped. I did it. I actually asked him for a date. But to cover myself, I added, ''It'll be more research on my book.''

Lowell dropped his head slightly. ''Sure. You need to get the feel of the land as well as the river.''

''Yes, that's it.''

Sunday afternoon was hot, as usual, but there was a breeze that made it bearable. In our jogging shoes, shorts, and T-shirts, we scrambled over rocky ridges and down steep hillsides. It had been so long since I had explored here with Merl that I didn't recognize anything. The trees were taller, the brush thicker than I remembered from my childhood. And surely a whole generation of new rocks had appeared!

This time I marveled at the variety of plant life, moist hidden havens of mosses and ferns in low places and on ridges and hillsides, arid expanses of short grasses, and stunted bushes with rocky slabs and boulders everywhere. Surrounding these extremes were heavily wooded areas, so shady that Lowell didn't need his hat because the sun rarely reached the ground.

It was phenomenal. I was so thrilled with being with Lowell, with the natural sounds of cicadas, birds, and the breeze through the trees that I truly believed that I must be a character in one of my novels where I can make everything come out right. This summer, for the first time in my adult life, I was actually living, not watching other people live. I wasn't experiencing life vicariously through my characters. And I loved it. It wasn't scary anymore. I didn't turn into a pumpkin. I reveled in it. As I tramped behind Lowell up a rocky trail, I wondered when I had begun living. The answer was easy; at my grandparents' funeral. Just over six weeks ago.

Laughing, we reached the crest of the hill, which turned out to be a bluff overlooking the river. We sat close together on a limestone rock crag, our bare legs dangling in the air. Below us was the river, continuing its ceaseless journey to the sea. Someone said you can't step twice into the same river. Here the water was deep in the quiet eddy and clear from the spring water that emptied into it just around the bend out of our view. It looked nothing like the murky river at the bridge.

It seemed only natural that Lowell should put his arm around me and pull me closer to him. I rested my head on his shoulder.

"It's beautiful," I said, memorizing the view to use in my novel. My Frenchman would use this as a lookout.

"Yes." Lowell's voice was soft and full of wonder.

His arm around my waist tightened a bit, making it very difficult for me to keep my mind on my mountain man and Dancing Star. I could see them fleeing from the Shawnees they spotted from this lookout. Forced by the British to move from their lands in the East, the Shawnees were invading the lands of the Osages. This could be the lookout where they watched for the enemy.

But the hum from the interstate, and an airplane leaving a vapor trail in the sky, told me it was not the eighteenth century. Lowell, leaning over, looked into my eyes, tilted my chin up with his finger, and kissed me. That long-ago time completely vanished from my thoughts as I kissed him back. We sat there for several minutes soaking up our enjoyment of each other's presence.

From our bluff we also had an unobstructed view into the rough land behind us. I thought I glimpsed the elusive wisp of mist I'd seen a few times. "Look." I pointed it out to Lowell. "What's that over there? Is it real, or just some light reflections?"

His eyebrows contracted as he studied it as it wavered and disappeared, so that we weren't sure we actually saw anything. "I don't know. An illusion, maybe? Or vapor off some water, but it couldn't be that. There's no water over there. Not even a spring."

"The phantom of Merryman's Crossing," I teased.

He stood up to see better. Nothing. "Let's take a closer look. Want to?"

I had trouble keeping up with him as he hurried down one hill and climbed another.

"I know where it came from," he said. "I saw some trees I'll recognize when we get nearer."

We paused in a glenlike area. "Whatever we saw came from here, somewhere," he said.

I didn't see any column of mist, or anything different from the land we'd come over. "Perhaps the sun shining at a certain angle caused an illusion," I suggested.

"Probably. Here's one of the trees I saw," he said pointing to a tall white oak, "and here's the other." He walked about ten yards to his left to a black walnut. I looked up into the canopy of leaves and saw it was loaded with green nuts. I made a mental note to come nutting in the fall.

"Let's look around." He paced back and forth under the walnut, searching the ground. I did the same near the oak.

His area was fairly level and covered with bluegrass, almost like a lawn. Easy to walk on. Mine was rocky, covered with buckbrush and vines. I had to watch out for poison ivy, which was plentiful. To avoid a patch of poison ivy, I climbed over a series of big rocks and boulders.

Most of the boulders were close together, making it easy to step from one to the other. I stopped at one place to judge whether I could jump. The next boulder was about three feet away. Its surface was mossy and damp, with no good place to land. I backed off the rock. The ground seemed safer here. A cool stream of air coming from between the boulders hit my face. I smelled a moist, earthy scent, not unlike Grandma's cellar under the store.

"Look here, Lowell," I said, carefully avoiding the poison ivy to look into the space between the rocks.

The cleft between the rocks narrowed to about sixteen inches wide and extended down into the ground about five feet.

"Move back very carefully," Lowell said, his voice pitched higher than usual. He sniffed the cool, humid air coming from the abyss. He tested the rock I had been standing on. It didn't move. "It's solid," he said, climbing on it. I scrambled after him. "I think you've discovered the mouth of a cave!" It looked like a deep pit to me, just space between two huge rocks.

"This must be where the vapor comes from," Lowell said, his face animated. "There could be a fissure down there leading into a cave. The air in caves is a constant fifty-six degrees. Maybe when this air we feel here—" He put out his hand to touch the difference between the air issuing from the fissure and the hot, dry air of mid-July. "—hits the surface air, it might create the mistlike effect we saw."

"Cool!"

I climbed onto the bigger boulder to get a different

perspective of the hole. "I don't see any mist here now."

"No, that's strange."

"Maybe it's magic!" I grinned at him to show that I was teasing. "Maybe the mist rose up to show us something, like buried treasure."

"Yeah, yeah." He moved his head from side to side, laughing at my imagination. "Or maybe it's a lure to entrap us. Whisk us away from our families."

"Or . . ." I slipped on the moist surface, sitting down abruptly. Lowell reached over the gap between the boulders in an attempt to grab me. He couldn't reach me. No problem. I was anchored solidly, though some dirt and rocks tumbled down into the space between us. We could hear the pebbles hit the bottom not far down.

"Or maybe it's just a place to show how awkward I am." I laughed. Closer to the edge, I peered down into the cleft. "It's not deep. Let's investigate." I looked for handholds to ease myself down, but seeing none, I decided I could slide down.

Lowell held back. "No, no, I don't think we should."

"Why not?" I didn't pay much attention to him. I was excited. Maybe we discovered something on my land that no one knew about. Not even my mountain man, Henri. The fact that he was fictional didn't occur to me. He was an explorer and so alive to me that I was in competition with him.

"I'm going down in," I said. I ignored Lowell's

garbled "Don't do it" because I could see the bottom, easily accessible just five feet down in the hole. Putting my feet out in front of me, with my hands pressed at both sides against the rock, I let myself slide down off the boulder. Then with a plonk, I landed feet first onto solid rock. The top of my head was even with the smaller boulder Lowell was standing on.

"Hey! This is super!" I had just enough room to squat and peer into the cool, moist darkness in front of me. I saw an opening big enough to squeeze through. Beyond that seemed to be a channel leading off horizontally from me, but I couldn't see much past the dim outline of the opening.

"Lowell," still squatting, I called up to him, "there's a hole here. Do you suppose it opens up into a cave?" He was kneeling on his boulder, just about three feet above me. I saw his face, dripping with perspiration, staring down at me. "Here." I stood up and extended my hand to him. "Help me back out." With a heave, he lifted me out of the cool space between the two boulders up beside him into the hot air.

"We need a light of some kind," I said, wondering why he was trembling. I was too keyed up to notice anything but the cleft in the rocks that led to a cave. "Let's go back to the store and get some flashlights."

Since we were less than a quarter of a mile from the store, I headed straight there through the underbrush, not looking for paths or easier footing. Then I stopped and turned around. I wanted to remember the spot so I could come back, but I was sure that Lowell knew the way, since he recognized the two trees that were taller than others near them. Even though I hadn't been running much recently, I was still in good shape. I easily outdistanced Lowell, grabbed two of the most powerful flashlights I had from the shelf in the store, and was back out on the porch when Lowell arrived.

"C'mon, slowpoke," I said, snatching his hand and starting back.

He put his hand on my arm to stop me. "It's getting late," he said. "Maybe we better leave this for another time."

His comment surprised me. He wasn't at all like the man who took me on the float trip to help me experience the river. Or even the man who started this excursion with me into the woods, climbing over rocks, and sitting precariously on the edge of the cliff looking down a hundred feet to the river. During the float on the river he was game for anything, even plowing onto the bridge with the swiftly running water as if it were a child's wading pool. I didn't understand his hesitancy.

"Aw, c'mon. It's only three o'clock. Lots of time."

I didn't give him an opportunity to answer, but I handed him one of the flashlights and ran back up the hill toward the tall oak tree. I didn't look to see if he followed, and I really didn't care. I wanted to see what kind of cave we'd discovered. When I did turn around, he was doing something at the door. Then he ran to catch up.

"Wait up, Kay," he called. "Wait for me before going back down that hole."

"Okay," I said, pausing to let him catch up. "Isn't this exciting?"

He shrugged, but kept on coming.

I was living. Man, I was really living! And I was at the same time creating a scene for my novel. In this wonderful place that my grandparents gave me, I was merging my real existence with my imaginary ones. Finding an unknown hideout was just exactly what I needed to advance my plot. I didn't even know before today that I needed a hideout, but here it was, handed to me on a . . . I started to say silver . . . on a rock platter. It was exactly what I needed to work up to the climax of my story. And perhaps even in my own life? I took Lowell's hand when he reached my side. His eyes were determined; the fear I had noticed earlier was gone.

"If you must go down in, Kay, I'm right here." He had difficulty saying this. I knew he didn't want to join me, but I was too charged up to wonder why.

Delighted, I kissed his cheek and slid once again into the narrow ravine between the boulders. "There's room for both of us," I said, motioning him to join me.

With his face set, the flashlight already lit in his hand, Lowell nodded but did not move.

Chapter Eight

The opening led off at a right angle. Just beyond, my flashlight played on open space.

"The passage looks big enough," I called up to Lowell, whose set face peered down on me. "I'm crawling through. As soon as I do, you come on down." I was on my hands and knees, ready to get through the passage. I wished I wore jeans to protect my knees from the gummy clay floor.

"Wait for me," he said. Some pebbles sprinkled down on my back as he positioned himself to slide in feet first.

I crawled through the short passage—actually it was more like a thick doorway—into a room large enough for me to stand almost erect. I swung my light around quickly to see that I had entered a low, narrow room.

"Hey, it's great!" I called back. My voice echoed

on the rock walls. "Come on. Once you get in here, there's room for both of us to stand up. And it's so cool!" I raised to my full height and struck my head on the rough ceiling. "Well, we can't stand up all the way. But, Lowell, it's perfect."

I expected him to join me and be as thrilled as I was at finding this pristine cave. Leaning over slightly to avoid hitting my head again, I took several steps into the cave. In the beam of my light, and the reflection of the light that glowed through the mouth at the bottom of the chasm, I saw the entire room.

The floor was smooth, hard-packed clay and rock, as if it was an ancient waterway. The limestone walls were layered and irregular like other caves in the area. On the ceiling were little soda straw stalactites. I didn't see any passageways leading off, but I intended to search thoroughly. I was sure there must be other passages.

What a perfect hideout! Dancing Star would certainly know of this cave. He and Henri could easily elude the Shawnee warriors. In my eagerness, I studied the space, wishing for paper and pencil to take notes.

Lowell still didn't come. I returned to the entrance, got on my hands and knees to stick my head out, and looked up. Lowell was still on his boulder, poised feet first, ready to slide down off his boulder, with both hands firmly planted beside him holding him in place.

"It's just one room as far as I can tell. Are you coming?"

"Yes," he said. He lifted up his hands to let his

body slide down the smooth rock side and landed in front of me on his feet. He was tall enough that his head was still aboveground. He maneuvered his tall body around so that he could squat down to see inside.

"How much room is there inside?" he asked.

"Lots. About six by fifteen feet or so. Come on in."

His face was dripping with perspiration as he scooted in feet first. He cautiously stood up and bumped his head. Groaning and rubbing it, he bent over and took a few steps toward me. His hand passed over a rock jutting out of the wall about two feet from the floor. He patted it and sat down.

"I'll let you do the exploring," he said. "How far back does the passage go?"

"I don't think any farther than we can see." I flicked my light to the back. The spotlight showed solid rock all around. "I don't see any passages leading out. I'll look."

By tilting my head slightly forward, I could walk upright. I circled the long, narrow room without finding any other opening large enough to crawl through. I did find a couple of fissures in the rocks and felt a draft through them.

"There must be more than this for such a strong draft to come out, don't you think?" I asked.

"Yes."

When I finished my inspection I looked at Lowell. He was backlighted by the natural light from the crawl hole we came through. His profile was silhouetted since he turned on his rocky seat, so he could see both me and the outside. He held himself rigid.

I was puzzled by his behavior, which was so different from when we had started out today. Then he had been jovial and ready for anything. Strange. Maybe that kiss turned him off? Perhaps we went too far and he was regretting it?

"Kay," he said after a long pause. "Are you afraid of anything?"

"Huh?"

"I mean do you have any phobias?"

"Oh. You mean besides talking into mikes in front of crowds of people?"

His laughter at my attempt at humor was forced. "No, I mean real fears."

"Well, I'm afraid of storms. Or I used to be. I don't think I am anymore."

"How come?"

"Remember the storm at my grandparents' funeral? Well, all the time we were at the cemetery I saw it coming. Even at the funeral home, I knew the wind was rising and was scared to death that it would storm. I couldn't listen to the preacher since I was worrying about the storm. Then after everything was over and we got back into the limo, I wasn't afraid anymore. It was as if the storm heralded Grandpa and Grandma's leaving. And from that time on they wouldn't let anything happen to me. We've had a couple of thunderstorms since then, and I didn't care. No, I don't have a phobia."

I'd been so wrapped up in my own thrill at finding the cave and plotting what I would do with this experience into my novel that I hadn't thought about Lowell. His trembling, excessive perspiration, and change of voice when I insisted on going into the cave all made sense. He was claustrophobic.

"Oh, I'm sorry, Lowell." I reached his side and laid my hand on his arm. "Why didn't you tell me you can't stand closed-in places?"

"I thought I could handle it. It's a silly thing. I know that nothing can harm me, but when I get into tight spaces, I can't stand it. I have to get out."

"And I made you come in here."

"No, I determined that I would get over it. See," he said, waving his arm to encompass the cave, "I am actually inside the earth. It surrounds me, not only below and on all sides, but it is *above* me. And I'm not a basket case. I think I'll be all right now. Like you with the storm. Your grandparents' spirits surrounding you took away your fear. Your presence here beside me sort of does the same thing. I'm tolerating it. I'm all right."

"Do you want to go outside? We can. I've seen what I wanted in here."

"No. Let's sit here for a while longer. Did you notice that we can't hear the traffic from the interstate in here?"

That was true. There was not a sound, except an occasional splat when a drop of water fell from the ceiling.

"No one else in the whole world knows about this cave," he continued.

"And if we got lost, no one would know where to look for us." That idea intrigued me and scared me at the same time. Good thing there weren't any further passages or I'd probably insist on crawling into them."

"Let's not think of that." He looked at the comforting daylight that glowed at the entrance. "But seriously, Kay, we could outlast an atomic attack here."

"There's plenty of water," I said, shining my light on the droplets coming from the ceiling and congregating in little pools on the floor.

"And we could live on the bats and lizards," he said, teasing me, yet shuddering and laughing at the thought. The old Lowell was back.

"We'd be the only people left on earth," I said, "safe and snug in our hideout."

"And when it was all over, we could repopulate the world."

That thought sobered me.

"Do you suppose anyone else has ever been in here besides us?" I asked.

"Not that I know. If anyone knew of it, I'd surely have heard, as much as I explored these hills as a kid. But come to think of it, I do remember seeing that mist a few times, but I never was curious about it. Because of the river and the springs, mist often hugs the ground all around here in the early mornings. No one ever wondered about it. New to the place, and trained to observe everything, you noticed it along with everything else here. And then it took your inquisitive mind and imagination to look for it.''

''And my stubbornness not to give up?''

''Yeah, that too.''

I kept thinking about Dancing Star. ''What about the Osages? Do you think they were ever in here?''

''Maybe. Or before them, the Ozark Bluff Dwellers, more likely. Let's look around to see what we can find on the floor here.''

As if we were on the forest floor instead of beneath it, Lowell suggested in his normal voice, ''You look there.'' He waved his arm back in the cave. ''And I'll search here nearer the opening.'' When I grinned at him for choosing the area closer to the light, he said, ''Well, maybe I'm not completely cured.''

Squatting down, he sifted through remains of leaves and debris washed or blown in. The floor where I searched was rocky with winding paths of clay and pebbles. I found some small animal bones, probably raccoon, Lowell said. There were lots of small rocks. ''Look for flint,'' he said.

''How can I tell it?'' I knew what he was thinking. Arrowheads or other stone tools would be evidence of Indians being here.

''Flint is harder and finer-grained than the sandstone or limestone. It's brighter in color, with smooth spots on it. Also look for pieces of pottery.''

Just then I picked up a rock I knew immediately was flint. Too big to be an arrowhead, it was shaped more like a scraper. One side was rounded, but the other edge, though broken, was serrated.

Young Dancing Star was here! He did make this his hideout! Or he could have, I amended, since he was not real.

I held the scraper up and shone my light on it so Lowell could see it. Even though I was as far back in the cave as I could go, he came to me and took it out of my hands. "We aren't the first people to be here." He studied the rock, turning it over and over, running his fingers over the tooth-like markings. This looks like it's from the Bluff Dweller era."

"Wow!"

Lowell was as excited as I was. "I'm betting that smaller boulder out there that hides the opening was pushed there ages ago by these people, just to make this a secure place."

I doubted that because the boulder looked much too large to be moved by humans. "Or maybe an earth-quake moved it?" I suggested.

"Could be. Whatever, we know for sure that some Indians used this cave."

We both sat down on the damp earth, digging in the clay with our fingers for more items. We had barely started when I said, "Let's don't disturb this."

"I agree. Let's leave it just as it is." He pointed his light in my face to see my expression. "I'm guessing that you are already plotting this into your novel, aren't you?"

"I'm way ahead of you. I've been doing that before we even found the cave."

"But you're not as completely lost in your story on this hike as you were on the river."

"No. I'm being me most of the time today."

"I like you being you."

We crawled out the hole and scrambled up the boulders to get out of the chasm. Without someone on top to pull us out, it was difficult to scale the smooth, rounded rock surface. Lowell boosted me up first. Then I gave him a hand to help him out. On top of the smaller of the two boulders, we looked down at where we had just been. There was nothing to suggest that there was a cave down there. Our footprints did not show on the rocky surface. All that indicated human passage was some moss knocked off the north side of the smaller boulder. It would have taken the tracking skills of Dancing Star's chief to know anyone passed this way.

We heard the drone of the cicadas. The hum from the interstate was like an undertone to the breeze through the leaves of the oak tree. An early, probably faulty, green walnut plopped down nearby.

The hot breeze tickled my cool cheek. I felt brand-new, as if I had just been born into the busy world. At the same time, I felt very ancient, as if I were one of the early peoples who sheltered in the cave. "Let's not tell anybody," I said.

"No, let's not. Then whatever happens, however much the world boxes us in, we'll know this exists."

"Yes, our beautiful secret." Lowell's words reminded me of one of the poems Mom made us memorize in English class. "The world is too much with us, late and soon . . ." I started quoting.

"Getting and spending, we lay waste our powers," Lowell quoted the next line.

"Little we see in Nature that is ours . . ." I broke in and looked at him in amazement.

"I had your mother as a teacher also."

"Oh!" Of course. I should have known. Mom had been teaching for many years at the high school. Most kids had at least one class with her before they graduated. But since Lowell was enough years ahead of me that he graduated before I started, I didn't think about him going to the same school.

"I liked another of Wordsworth's poems better," he said. "And it also fits today."

"Which one?"

He looked steadily at me as he quoted, "She was a phantom of delight, when first she gleamed upon my sight." He didn't have to tell me that he was thinking of me. I also remembered that poem and the phrase that came after, "A lovely apparition."

"Only I think of the 'apparition' in the poem not being a spirit, but a jewel," he said. "Not flashy like gold or diamonds. Not even shiny like silver. More opaque, mysterious, and perfectly formed by nature, not by an artisan's skill. A jewel like a pearl."

I was becoming embarrassed again. He obviously knew my first name because the lawyer said it during the reading of the will, and because I made such a big deal about Dad not calling me Pearlie Kay. He was giving me the finest compliment I'd ever received. I didn't know why I was ill at ease. But whenever he started complimenting me or showing interest, I wished I was someplace else. Probably because I wasn't used to it and didn't know how to act. Remember, until just recently, I didn't live except through my characters. I couldn't throw off that veil so quickly.

"Pearl is a beautiful name," he said, "and fits you perfectly."

Luckily I didn't have to respond that I'd always hated that name. But if he liked it, maybe . . .

A car horn blared from the store. A man's voice yelled my name several times. "It's Merl," I said to Lowell.

As if caught in something illegal, we both jumped off the boulder and ran down the hill to the store. "We're up here, Merl," I yelled. I saw Vivian standing by Merl's car.

"I completely forgot," Lowell said, groaning and shaking his head in dismay. "Merl and Vivian said they'd be by this afternoon to start decorating for their wedding. I've got to let them in the schoolhouse."

"Sorry," he said when Merl joined us on the path above the store. "I forgot."

Merl looked at the two of us, our hair disheveled and our bare arms and legs smeared with cave clay. He smiled knowingly. "I can see you've been busy," he teased.

"We just went on a walk." When he grinned even more, I added, "It's no big deal. Don't get all bent out of shape. I wanted to see the rest of the land that goes with the store and asked Lowell to go with me."

"Sure, I know. More research, huh?"

"That's right." By now we were at the store and greeted Vivian.

"When you didn't show up at the schoolhouse," Vivian said to Lowell, "we came to the store and found your note fastened to the door."

I reached out to take the note. "Gone exploring by the big oak tree," the note said in a hastily scrawled hand. I looked at Lowell. He shook his head just enough to warn me not to say more. Then I understood. He put the note on the door when we came back to get the flashlights. With his fear of caves, he left it in case we got lost in the cave.

"That was thoughtful of you, Lowell," Vivian said, "to let us know where to find you. Otherwise we might have made a useless trip."

Lowell didn't tell her the real reason he left the note, but flashing a quick grin at me, accepted her approval.

Lowell led the way to the schoolhouse and unlocked the door. No matter that it had been years since the building was used as a school, it still smelled of chalk, oiled floor, wood smoke, and children's lunches. Or at least my imagination smelled it.

A couple of cars pulled up back at the store. I groaned and pretended I didn't see them. People piled out of the cars and walked up the porch, looking and exclaiming at everything. They were obviously tourists. When the door didn't open, they walked over to the blacksmith and peered in the dirty windows.

"The store's closed," I yelled to them from the schoolhouse door. "It'll be open tomorrow."

One older couple came to me. "We heard about the store and came specially to see it," the woman said, disappointed.

"Yes," her husband said, "all the way from Minneapolis. Do you know where the manager is? Do you suppose he could open up for us?"

"I'm the owner," I said. "I'll let you in." I didn't want to. I hated having to leave the schoolhouse. I wanted to be in on the wedding plans. Also I didn't want to cut into my time with Lowell. But I had a business to run. If I wanted to lure in tourists, I'd have to be flexible.

When the two cars left, after the people purchased over two hundred dollars worth of crafts and snacks, Lowell had gone home. Merl and Vivian honked good-bye as they drove by on their way back to town.

I sat all by myself on the porch step. The oppressive heat of the day was easing some. The whiffs of cooling breeze off the river didn't compensate for the letdown I felt at the ending of such a wonderful day. A day that brought Lowell and me closer. The day we discovered a secret cave, and Merl and Vivian decorated the schoolhouse for their wedding. I felt cheated that I had to skip the ending. I decided right then that I'd pay whatever necessary to hire someone to help me in the store. This one incident convinced me it would be worth it.

My new awareness of life was overwhelming me— Lowell, the store, my writing. A deadline was looming and I was not ready.

I'll call Maria, I decided. Immediately, I felt better. With her help, I could do it all. After I showered and changed clothes, the telephone rang. It was Lowell. All was right with my world.

Chapter Nine

O nce again I was crying at a family gathering. Only this time it wasn't at the end of my grandparents' togetherness, but the beginning of Merl and Vivian's. I was crying because the schoolhouse looked so right with Vivian's simple touches that magically transformed the room into a wedding chapel. I was crying because Merl was so handsome in his light tan slacks and white silk shirt that matched the colors in Vivian's street-length dress. I was crying because the house was filled to overflowing with well-wishing relatives, friends, and neighbors. Because Merl and Vivian were right for each other. And because the spirits of my grandparents were in the room, engulfing all of us and promising to their eldest grandson and his bride a life as happy and productive as theirs.

When I thought I was sated with emotions, another

feeling completely overwhelmed me. Merl and Vivian each said, "I do." The preacher pronounced them husband and wife, and gave them permission to kiss. Quietly at first, almost like a whisper, and then gradually growing stronger as the kiss continued, came Lowell's deep voice filling the room with a happy melody.

> From now on, my friends,
> Your lives flow together.
> Even death cannot part you
> From your love forever.
>
> For years you have loved
> With eyes for no other.
> Walk home now as one
> Your life is forever.

All eyes were on Merl and Vivian. Lowell wasn't up front with them. I had to turn to see him in the back of the room, standing between the table piled with gifts and the reception table with the tiered cake topped with Clyde's carved bride and groom. Lowell's voice filled the room. Nobody moved. There was not a cough or murmur as the bride and groom were locked in their embrace, surrounded by the vibrations of Lowell's song. His voice held and trilled on the last word, just as it had at the funeral on the word, "gone." But this three syllable word ended with a happy lilt. Lowell sang "for-ev-er," with an uplift at the last note. Then silence. We wanted to clap but didn't think that was appropriate.

With perfect timing, Merl and Vivian broke from the kiss and faced the audience. His arm around Vivian, Merl looked over the crowd, catching individual eyes. He paused longer at me than anyone else. And winked, or so it seemed to me. Still facing Merl, Vivian was radiant.

When he finished his survey of the room, ending with a nod of appreciation to Lowell, Merl said, ''Now, let's eat.''

''Yes,'' Vivian said, almost giggling, and looked up at us for the first time. It was as if she were suddenly aware that she had guests and remembered her manners. ''Won't you join us?''

It took a few seconds for us to switch from the seriousness of the ceremony and Lowell's song to the lighter tones of their invitation. Seated beside me, Dwight quipped, ''It's about time!''

Someone else said, ''Thought you'd never ask.''

''Lands sakes, yes, child,'' Nora said. ''I can't wait to taste that cake you baked.'' Then she hurried back to the table to help with the serving.

''Lead on,'' Uncle Bruce said, standing and pulling Aunt Betsy up beside him, ''before all the sherbert in the punch melts.''

With his arm around her waist, Merl escorted Vivian down the narrow aisle that was strung with ribbons to match the colors in their outfits. They laughed and greeted friends as they went. It took several minutes for them to reach the reception table amid all the congratulations and their responses. Then followed the usual cutting of the cake and serving punch and nuts.

I stayed in the background, reverting to my accustomed role as observer. Or I tried to be invisible until Lowell joined me.

"That song was beautiful," I said.

"I wrote it for them," he said in his soft voice that I had to strain to hear. "But I hoped you'd like it."

"It's different from the one you sang for my grandparents."

"Different occasion."

"Each of them caught the mood perfectly."

Lowell's lips turned up at the corners in pleasure.

"One sad and one happy, yet they both celebrate love," I added. "The end of love that endured for a lifetime and the beginning of another love that will last a lifetime."

"I hoped you'd see that." He clutched my hand.

I studied this man of contradictions. With the soul of a poet, an accomplished musician, a visionary, and a nature lover, how could he be so blind to human frailty? How could he be so set in his views? Ruining young people's lives to enforce some outdated notion?

I watched Dwight at the table teasing Merl and Vivian as they shared their slice of cake. Dwight glanced at Shannon and smiled but did not go to her. Even though they were across the room from each other, like at Romeo and Juliet's first meeting, I sensed the sparks between them. But Dwight was the model of decorum. He stayed away, and she didn't come to the table until he went outside. I suspected he intended to decorate Merl's car for he motioned to a few other guys to join him.

Lowell glanced at Dwight a time or two, but when he saw he was not going to Shannon, he stopped watching. The usual frown on his face when he looked at my brother was not there this time, though his face was serious.

Maria hurried by me, chasing her little boy. When he turned back, escaping her arms, I grabbed him. Laughing, I said to him, ''Whoa there, Bobby. You'll bump into something. Say, how about me getting you some cake?''

''He's been begging for it,'' Maria said, ''but I didn't want to push in line.''

''Well, Bobby, c'mon, let's get you some.''

I cut a slice with extra icing on it and dipped out a cup of punch, making sure there was some sherbert floating in it. Since there was no place for a child to eat inside, I took him outside to sit at one of the desks that had been moved out temporarily to make room for the wedding.

''He likes you,'' Maria said. ''He keeps talking about that nice lady in Olen's store.''

''My name is Kay, Bobby.'' He didn't answer for he was busy stuffing his mouth full of cake.

I was surprised he even remembered me for all I'd done was wave at him when his mother stopped by the store each morning. She rarely brought him in. Sometimes I sent a toy or cookie out to him with his mother. The few times he was in the store, Maria kept a close tether on him.

"He misses being in the store," Maria said. "Before I got the job at the rest home in town, I sometimes helped Olen out. Especially after Faith got so bad. We put a playpen in the corner. Of course, that was when he was smaller." She looked at the active little boy. "That wouldn't work now."

I couldn't believe how everything was working out. I was just thinking about asking her. "I've been wanting to talk to you about working in the store, and I didn't even know that you had worked for my grandfather. I really need someone to relieve me, so I can meet my writing deadlines. The business has grown so since I've been here that I can rarely get away. Even on Sunday and evenings there's often someone wanting in." I watched her reaction. She was taking in every word I said, her eyes bright. "I'm thinking of keeping the store open longer. I don't know what you make in town, but taking out what you have to pay a baby-sitter because you could keep Bobby with you in the store, I might be able to match what you bring home. Interested?"

"I'll say I'm interested. That would be great. My car is getting old and needs lots of work, or I'll have to trade for a better one. That doesn't even include the gas I have to buy to drive forty miles a day." She was as excited as I was. "Do you think it's possible?"

"I think so."

A big part of the load I'd carried since I'd learned I inherited the store lifted. I saw some relief. I could spend at least half of every day writing. That was all the time I ever spent, anyway. To make it financially possible, all I had to clear from the store was what I'd been getting part time at the convenience store in the city. Even less because now I didn't have to pay rent. And then there were the advances from the contracts on the young people's historical series I was sure to get if I finished the first one on time. I could do that. The store was making money. With Maria there, I'd still be the one who operated the store as the grand-parents wanted.

"When could you start?"

"Right away, probably. I need to give a week's no-tice, but I could come tomorrow as it's Sunday, and next week for a couple of hours each day after I get home."

"Wonderful. Come by later this evening when everything's over. We'll work out the details."

"Hey, Kay, Maria, all you guys out there," Dwight yelled to us from the schoolhouse. "Come on in. Vi-vian's about to throw the bouquet."

Everyone who was outside trooped back in. Vivian was standing on the platform, swinging her spray of white carnations back and forth.

"Come on, let 'er rip," Dad said.

Enjoying her role, Vivian waited until all the girls and young women were gathered around her.

"Turn around," Nora said. "Let's be fair here. No favorites."

"Close your eyes," Aunt Betsy said.

Obediently Vivian turned around. She closed her eyes tight, paused a second, and holding the spray in both hands, tossed it over her shoulder. It arched up, almost hitting the ceiling and landed right in Shannon's hands. Everyone clapped and cheered except Lowell.

"Oh, no," he said, his face stricken.

Get real, man. This doesn't mean anything. Surely you're not superstitious. I wanted to yell this out, but held my tongue.

Shannon stared at the bouquet in surprise. Then she looked at me. "I shouldn't have this. I'm going to college next month, and it will be at least four years before I'll think of marrying. Here, Kay." She put it in my hands. "It's yours."

The room exploded with laughter and cheers. Vivian said to me loud enough that most people heard her, "I thought I was throwing it at you, anyway."

Merl and Dwight clapped me on my back hard enough that I flinched. Chet did his jig around me. Dad and Mom grinned. I didn't dare look at Lowell.

The hubbub around me distracted the attention from the bride and groom. Merl took this opportunity to grab Vivian's hand. They ran out the door before Dwight yelled, "They're getting away!"

With their headstart, they were in the car before anyone reached them. We burst out the door to throw bird seed at them and shout congratulations. Merl took off. Strings of cans rattled on the gravel behind him. The cloud of dust his wheels stirred up almost hid the "Just Married" scrawled on the back window.

We stood there in the middle of the road watching Merl's car cross the bridge and disappear up the grade on the other side. *Everything is working out just as you planned, Grandpa and Grandma. The music parties are continuing, Dwight is going to college, and Merl and Vivian's house is almost finished. Finally they are married.*

I could almost hear Grandma answering while her busy fingers pieced together another quilt block, "Now it's your turn, Pearl Katherine." She always called me by both names.

"Give her time, Faith," Grandpa would say. "She'll do all right. I'm still not sure we did the right thing for her. I hope we did, but, Granddaughter . . ." He'd turn to me with a serious expression in his blue eyes. "I hope you take the store, but remember that you don't have to."

I wished I could tell them that I was fine. I, like my brother and cousin, just needed the shove or incentive that they gave us. I would go my own way. I wasn't forced to stay.

I looked across the lawn at my store. I should get over there and unlock it, as some of the people at the wedding might need to get something. MERRYMAN'S STORE, my bright new sign proclaimed in tall red-and-black letters. The antique gas pump, shining red, was a beacon for me as well as for tourists who pulled off the interstate. The new coat of white paint on the store glistened in the low rays of the sun. Filtering through the trees bordering the river, the sun's reflection on the double windows on either side of the door was like giant eyes welcoming me.

So comforting and so much a part of the landscape was the store that I didn't worry about the black clouds in the west. The wedding was over, and the men had just finished moving the desks back inside the school where the women were clearing up. A cool change in the air promised a thunderstorm. The wind picked up a paper napkin that dipped and gyrated until it lodged against the porch. I didn't care if it stormed. The store had stood there over a hundred years. Nothing would harm it. Faith and Olen wouldn't allow it.

Lowell came behind me and put his arm around my waist. "Beautiful, isn't it?" I said.

"Yes. And so are you."

There was that embarrassment again at his compliments. So as usual, I changed the subject. "I'd like to say something to my grandparents right now."

"What would you say?"

The spirit that always seemed near me seemed to be just over my head. I listened to the murmur of voices at the schoolhouse, the drone from the highway, and the nearer rustle of the wind through the trees. I couldn't actually hear it, but I imagined just how the river sounded as it lapped across the bridge.

Lowell prompted me again, "What would you say, Kay?"

The sun crept behind the cloud. The magic windows reverted to ordinary glass through which I could see the contents of the store. Behind the three upstairs windows, I visualized my belongings that were mingled with my grandparents' things.

"I'd say, 'Grandpa and Grandma, thanks for giving me Merryman's Crossing. No one ever received such a bequest before.' And then, Lowell, I'd tell Grandpa, 'Don't worry, I want to.' "

Lowell's arms tightened around me. I took his hands in mine and squeezed them.

Chapter Ten

Maria's working in the store was a godsend. I opened the store each day, then at nine o'clock when Maria came, I buried myself in my study with my computer until late afternoon. I took over from then until we closed after the last customer left. The first couple of Sundays we were open were slow, but gradually as people learned we were open, trade picked up enough to make it worthwhile.

Dwight was the one to point out to me why I choose those particular hours to be in the store. I thought those were hours that would best fit in with my writing schedule and help Maria work around Bobby's needs. "Yeah, yeah," he said, "you've fixed it so that you are in the store when Lowell stops by in the morning and again when he comes home." I started to object. "Don't tell me you're not serious about him."

I made a face at him. Maybe he was right. But I was the boss and could work when I wanted. I liked being an entrepreneur better all the time. Besides, not working a full eight hours each day, Maria could help out on weekends and still get in her forty hours a week. Being in the store when Lowell stopped by was just a lucky coincidence. Or so I convinced myself.

With Maria in the store, more local young people stopped by, often congregating in the library section. Now that the haying was done, Shannon spent more time in the store. I squeezed in some more chairs to make it more inviting. Invariably the kids spent money on drinks, snacks, and often more substantial groceries to take home. As Shannon predicted, the rental video section did a good business.

Acoustics were bad in the store building. From my office I heard voices and activity downstairs. Out of the window, when I looked up from my computer screen, I could see cars pull up to the store and watch the activity across the road at the blacksmith shop. But tuning out the noises below, I could concentrate on my work.

Sometimes, when I heard several people chatting in the library nook, I'd come down from my office with my latest chapter to read portions out loud. Steve and Clyde usually joined us when they heard me begin to read. And Chet also, when he wasn't in his shop. Nora was a frequent visitor. Soon my novel became a neighborhood effort, everyone suggesting ideas and giving me their reaction.

"That wouldn't work," Steve said when I read the scene when Henri first floats down the river by the Osage village. "You've got Dancing Star hiding in the bushes. In that time, the bottom land along the river would have been almost impassable with cane groves, not the brush we see now."

Shannon said, "Henri spoke French, so why not put in a few French phrases?"

"Yeah," Maria said, joining us when she wasn't busy with a customer, "and a few Osage words to make it more realistic."

Even Bobby sat quietly and listened. The middle school age level I was writing for was above his first grade level, but his attention to certain passages helped me know what was working.

Though I thought of those readings as breaks for me, they were actually polishing sessions. My editor complimented me on the chapters I sent her. She said they were the best writing I'd ever done for her. "You are really showing, not telling in your story now. I am there living with your characters. The air at your quaint Merryman's Crossing must be healthful."

I didn't tell her the air had very little to do with it. It was my grandparents and my neighbors who forced me out of the observer's role, so that I could put more feeling into the story. Especially one neighbor, but I didn't tell her about him.

My editor continued, "I'll soon send you a contract for a few more books about Dancing Star and Henri." Alone in my office talking to her on the phone, I couldn't do a jig like Chet, but I squeezed the fingers of my free hand into a fist and made a quick victory sign. I probably gave some audible response because she laughed and said, "That is if you are interested?"

Perfect. Absolutely perfect. For the next few years I was set. Contracts for books and Merryman's Store.

Another person I came to depend on was Nora. After finishing her dinner dishes, she often brought over her knitting. Some days she finished a pair of baby booties and set them on my handicraft shelf to sell. Maria especially appreciated her presence when tourists came, or when another tour bus pulled up.

True to her promise, the first tour guide director who had stopped sent me her schedule and also told a few others. We'd have a busload almost every week. Not a big breakthrough, but a start. Even if Nora wasn't already in the store, when a bus pulled up, she hurried over. I offered to pay her, but she waved me off with, "Lands sakes, child, gettin' paid for talkin'?"

"Most people would pay to shut her up," Steve teased her.

Classes at the university started the last week in August. Since Dwight had paid off his fines way ahead of schedule, he spent his last few days of vacation with me. He enjoyed visiting with the men on the porch about farming and ranching, as well as doing some fishing and hiking. I was tempted to tell him about the Secret Cave, but I didn't. That was Lowell and my special secret.

The storm that hit the night of Merl and Vivian's wedding was the beginning of a wet spell that lasted into August. The unusual moisture was the main topic of conversation among the men on the porch.

"The rains are good for the corn," Steve said.

"Yep," Clyde agreed, turning his latest carving over in his hands to see where he needed to work on it. "This last shower will make it."

"Hope it don't turn off dry after this," Chet said. "Soybeans need at least a couple more good soakings."

The other men agreed, even though none of them were actively farming anymore.

"River's comin' up," Steve said.

The other men nodded. That was nothing new. They had lived all their lives with the unpredictable river. They looked down the hill toward the bridge. Muddy water was rushing over the curbings, completely hiding the bridge. And, as would be expected, that day very few customers braved the water to come to the store. The people up our road crossed as usual. Activity at the courthouse must have increased, for Lowell stopped by as usual every morning on his way to work for his coffee and roll. His heavy pickup had no problem crossing against the current.

The last day of Dwight's vacation was a clear day, for a change. He borrowed Chet's canoe and Grandpa's fly rod to fish the eddy below the bridge. Though still higher than usual, the water flow was not dangerous, either over the bridge or in the eddy. After he left, I settled in to revise what I'd written the day before. Downstairs in the store, I heard Maria reading to Bobby. Then he went outside to play. From my office window I watched Chet open up the double doors of his shop. Bobby joined him. The two disappeared inside. The day promised to be sunny after several cloudy days.

At noon I fixed some sandwiches, picked out two cans of cold drink and hiked through my back woods to the river below the bridge. I thought I knew where I'd find Dwight, under the bluff where the spring emptied into the river. That was where I used to take him as a little boy when we visited the grandparents. On the rare times when Mom would let him come with Merl and me, he used to pester me until I gave in and took him to his spring.

He was there, sitting on a rock shelf overlooking the clear water that spewed up from the base of the bluff, boiling up into the brown, muddy river. His canoe was beached up river a few rods and tied to a sycamore tree. I climbed up onto the rock to sit beside him. He grinned at me when I handed him his lunch.

"I thought I'd find you here," I said.

"It's still my favorite place. I want to soak up all this to take it with me to college. I figure that by going year-round and taking a heavy load of classes, I can get my degree in three years."

"What's the hurry?"

He didn't answer but stared out over the bubbling spring below us and down the river where its muddy, hurtling current carried leaves and tree limbs on its crest. The strength of the spring water forced some beached logs back into the center. For several yards below the spring, the clear water fought with the river, mixing and diluting the river for as far as we could see. However, we knew that beyond that the stronger river swallowed the purer spring water.

We ate our sandwiches. Upriver we heard a car at the bridge. We watched Shannon's Chevy Cavalier creep across. Half of her wheels were hidden in water that looked to us as if it was at the bottom of her doors. Alarmed, we both stood up.

"She shouldn't cross in that little car," Dwight said, his voice trembling. He instinctively grabbed my hand like he used to do as a little boy.

"She's okay," I said, trying to alleviate his fears. "She crosses all the time. She understands the river and knows when it's safe."

"It doesn't look safe to me," Dwight said.

She reached the far side of the bridge. First the front wheels emerged, then the back ones. Dripping water, the Cavalier gathered speed as she drove it up the grade toward Highway M.

Dwight let out his breath. "The current is really strong today. I realized that the minute I put my canoe in up there at the bridge. I got to here and decided not to go farther. I can fish from the bluff. I don't want to end up sucked under some fallen log."

Was this my daredevil brother speaking?

"Got any bites?" I asked.

"Naw. River's no good. But fishing was just an excuse, anyway. I just wanted to get outside for a while before . . ." He didn't finish.

"Are you worried about college?"

"No, I'm excited. I know I can do it, but it'll be different. And lots harder than high school. I guess I'm scared. First time on my own and all that."

"Yeah, I know."

A log floated by. We watched it hurry downstream and catch on a tree at the riffle. The current forced it crossways where the water narrowed into a chute. Other debris caught on the log until within minutes there was a small dam. The water spiraled under it, stronger now because of the suction of the more restricted passageway.

The sun on us was hot but not uncomfortable because of the coolness from the spring. The river noise blocked out the rumble of interstate traffic, so that we seemed isolated, just brother and sister enjoying our lunch on the moss-covered rock overlooking the river.

"How does it feel to own all this?" Dwight asked.

"I still can't believe it."

"Believe it. It's all legally yours now. Signed, sealed, and delivered. So is my trust. But you didn't answer my question. How do you feel?"

"Powerful." The sky, the forests, the fields, the river. All mine! "And awed."

"Yeah, I know what you mean. The power of owning this place, this land. You can do what you want with it. It's yours. Yet you're scared of how great it is. How unreal it is that you can own a river?''

"Or a town?''

"Yes, a town. And guardian of the family heritage, don't forget that.''

"I haven't for a moment.''

He looked at me with awakened respect. "Awesome. I'm glad Grandpa and Grandma gave it to you.''

I'd never had such a conversation with Dwight before. For sure, I'd been away too long. It was time I was back. I hardly knew him, yet I had known his every movement from birth.

"You know, Dwight, I don't need to be the trustee of your scholarship. You are perfectly capable of handling it yourself. I'll tell the lawyer.''

"I appreciate your confidence in me, but remember what he said. We have to follow *everything* in the will, or it goes to Dad and Uncle Bruce. I want that trust, so you've got to be trustee for me. I hope it's not going to be any trouble for you.''

"No, no, not at all. It's not that. I'm happy to do it, but you seem so sure of where you're going now that I bet if Grandpa saw you, he wouldn't put that restriction on the money but give it straight out like he did for Merl.''

"Lots of things have changed since his death.''

"You said it.'' I was marveling at how Dwight had become a man, when I should have noticed how I'd become more responsible. I had grown up just as much as he in the past two-and-a-half months. I hardly resembled the person I was in my sterile apartment in the city, living only through my characters.

"Our grandparents sure were smart. They knew exactly what they were doing, didn't they?" I asked after a long pause when we watched the river.

"Yes, they did. The right thing for all of us."

"Even Lowell?"

Dwight didn't flinch. "Yes, even Lowell. He's kept the music parties going. I don't think you would have. So that's a good thing."

"Was it right for him, too?"

He thought for a few seconds. "Yes, I think so. Shannon wrote that when he's working with the music scholarship kids and the music parties that he's not on such a crusade. More human, you might say. More understanding."

"And," I prompted him when he stopped.

"And what?"

"And what do you think about him butting in about your fine?"

He didn't stiffen as he usually did when anyone mentioned his problem. "I've paid every last cent of that fine. Shannon writes that Lowell is softening his attitude toward me. She wants me to ease up, also."

"Well, can you?"

"I guess. It's history now. Last Friday the judge lifted the probation when I brought in the last payment. He was really impressed. I had two years to pay it, you know, and I did it all this summer."

"We're all proud of you. I believe that Grandpa and

Grandma somehow planned that, too. It's really scary how they seemed to program all of us to do just what we should.''

"Yeah, it is." He drew in his fishing line and tossed it farther out. "They couldn't have done it if they were alive."

"No, we wouldn't have listened to them. Even Merl wouldn't have accepted the money. He's too proud."

"I wouldn't have worked so hard this summer to pay it off without the trust being there for me when I start college. Before their death, I was mad and didn't care. I couldn't see the end, so why bother? I'd probably have done something else dumb, gotten into more trouble. But with the trust waiting for me, I felt good."

He took a deep breath. "Now I'm free, Kay, free. Dad and Mom are going to pay for my room and board because Mom said that was only fair. They paid yours. So I don't think I'll work any, even part time. That way I can take a heavy load and get out sooner. And have some of the trust left."

"And are you still mad at Lowell?"

"Well." He made a face. "I'm working on it. When Shannon and I get to college, I'm going to start seeing her again, not just writing letters. Lowell or no Lowell."

While we were talking it became cloudy. In the west on the headwaters of the river, a dark cloud with streaks of lightning showed there was a heavy storm over there.

"We better be getting back," I said, eyeing the clouds. Dwight pulled in his line.

I started to cut through the woods toward home. Dwight would paddle Chet's canoe back to the bridge.

"Hey," Dwight shouted when he climbed down the rocky bank to the canoe, "the river's rising fast!"

Alarmed, I turned back and climbed down to him. A big log tumbled over and over in the middle of the river, jamming into the one we saw earlier. Down the center of the river was a crest, which Grandpa told me indicated the water was rising. We didn't have to see that to know because the river was at least three inches higher on the rock ledge we had just vacated. The muddy surge of water rolling down the river almost drowned the clean, bubbling spring water.

Other limbs followed the big log. Styrofoam pieces bobbed on the surface foam. Aluminum cans cascaded by, along with other trash from careless people upstream. The sky in the west lightened, indicating the brief storm was over. Even though I wasn't afraid of storms anymore, I still gave a sigh of relief that the storm wore itself out before reaching us. I didn't want to be outside, wide open. I felt safe in the store, though not on a rocky ledge overlooking the river.

We pulled the canoe up the bank, farther out of the river, lifting it over some rocks and dragging it up a small ravine into a grassy area. When Dwight tied it securely to a dogwood tree above possible flood level, I turned from the river and once again started back to the store. A few drops of rain hit me even as the sun peeked out again. At least we were spared the storm, but it must have been a doozy upstream to send that avalanche of water down so quickly.

Dwight held back, mesmerized by the river rising before his eyes.

"Wow!" he said. "How can it rise so fast?"

"That storm upstream must have come so quickly that the water all ran off. Small rivers like this one can rise in minutes. Let's get back."

From the road on the far side of the bridge, I heard a car motor.

"Hey, wait," Dwight said, grabbing me, "that's Shannon's Cavalier. She's coming back." He barged through the brush and trees along the river in as straight a path as he could run toward the bridge. "Don't cross, Shannon," he yelled. "Stay there!"

I was on his heels. "She can't hear you this far away."

"Shannon!" Dwight screamed. He was waving his arms over his head and whooping as loud as he could to get her attention.

The front wheels of Shannon's Cavalier were about a foot from the water that rushed recklessly downstream. She paused on the road where it leveled out after descending the hill for the approach to the bridge.

We were close enough to see her through her lowered window. She was leaning out to get a better look at the river. There was a pile-up of logs on the upstream side of the bridge, forcing the current under and to the right around them, but they did not completely obstruct the way. Only some leafy, limber branches swayed in the pathway. Shannon must have decided that crossing was doable for she rolled up her window, turned on her windshield wipers, revved the motor a couple of times, and spinning gravel from her front wheels, charged onto the bridge with as much speed as the little car could give from a dead start. Water spewed up in huge waves on either side of her, blocking our view of her. The engine roared as she bolted across the flooded floor of the old concrete low-water bridge. Even the side curbings were invisible under the angry, muddy deluge.

''Shannon!'' Dwight screamed again, blind to the briars and poison ivy that blocked his path.

Right behind him I shrieked, ''Shannon!''

Chapter Eleven

Dwight and I stopped running when Shannon plowed steadily on across the bridge. We couldn't believe she would try to drive across. I was too shocked to do anything but stare.

"No!" Dwight yelled. His voice was drowned in the roar of the river and the whine of the Chevy's engine. The strong current slowed her momentum as she reached our side of the river. She shifted to low gear, gunned her engine, and forged on.

"She's made it!" Dwight cried in relief as her front wheels reached the place where we knew the bridge ended and the road fill began.

My heart beat rapidly from my fear and from running. Yet I couldn't help admire her driving skill and her nerve. This kind of stunt was more like something Dwight would do, yet even he recognized the danger.

Just when the car should have been safely on the road where it leveled out for about twenty feet before climbing the rise to the store, the front end suddenly nosedived and slipped into the brown water. The engine sputtered and died. We heard a sickening swish, or suction intake, as the river claimed the car. We watched in horror as the bronze current, racing around the bridge support, surged against the passenger side of her blue car. The Cavalier plunged into the main course of the flooded river. The current turned the car onto its left side and washed it downstream until it struck a submerged log right in front of us.

"Shannon!" Dwight screamed. He lunged toward the river ready to dive in.

"Wait!" I shouted, grabbing him.

My strength was nothing compared to his. He shook me off and waded out into the water. The current was stronger than he expected, for it pulled his feet out from under him. He went completely under, but since the water wasn't deep along the sloping bank where we stood, he quickly regained his balance. I pulled him back. Though it was a hot August day and the temperature of the water was tepid, he was shaking uncontrollably. So was I.

The spinning front wheel on the passenger side was still above water as the Chevy lay on its side. As we watched in horror, the car settled until it was completely covered; only the blue of the right fender was barely visible under several inches of opaque amber water. We couldn't see Shannon. She was trapped underwater in the car, probably lying on her left side and still holding to the steering wheel, hopefully protected by the air bag. Her Cavalier was laying on the bedrock of a flooding river that pinned it against a log!

"Wait!" I cried, both of my arms around Dwight, holding him back. This time if he went into the river, he'd take me with him. That stopped him. "Wait, I'll get the rope from the canoe. Keep you from washing down the river."

Dwight nodded, his eyes wild. We both knew he had to reach Shannon quickly. The rope would give him some protection from being washed away himself.

"I saw her roll up the window," I said, trying to reassure us both. "That means she has air." I yelled over my shoulder as I ran back to the canoe. "Wait for me."

I didn't hear his answer, but when I ran over the crest of the hill, I glanced back. Dwight was pacing the bank, studying it and the runaway current.

While I untied the rope from the canoe and ran back, I figured out what happened. The river, diverted from its usual path by the logjam against the bridge, turned its force toward the west bank and road fill. It swirled around the last concrete support of the bridge, washing away the rocks and dirt. Hidden under the brown surface was a watery gap where the road approach should be. Not seeing it, and knowing that she was safely across the bridge, Shannon accelerated when reaching the end of the bridge. Her car dropped right into the hole. Its speed must have slammed the bumper and radiator into the raw edge of the rocky fill.

I was back with the tie rope from the canoe in minutes, though it seemed hours. We tied one end around Dwight's waist. The rope was long enough that I looped the other end over a strong-looking branch of a young maple tree and for extra security, I held on to it as well. Calling Shannon's name, Dwight jumped into the river beside the overturned car. He went under, but then regained his feet and stood up, his head barely above water. To hold himself in place, he grabbed the nearest part of the car that he could hold on to, the flange of the right fender that was just a few inches underwater. Then, his feet kicking to keep the current from pushing him farther into the river, and me holding him in place with the rope, he tried to reach her. Hand over hand, holding on to any projection he could find on the car's undercarriage, he gradually moved down the length of the car to the passenger door. The riverbed slanted down, so that the farther he crawled along the car, the deeper the water was. He was completely underwater when he reached the passenger door. He popped up for air. Even standing on the right side of the overturned car, he was barely above water. He couldn't stay there; the current tried to wash him downstream. I had difficulty holding on to the rope.

He ducked underwater again to look in the window. When he came up for air, he said more hopefully, "I don't think there's any water inside."

Good. There should be enough air to last Shannon for a while. If the car didn't leak!

"Can you see her?"

"No, there's some bags and other stuff from the car in the way. It's too dark to see details."

"Is she okay?"

"Can't tell. I banged on the side to let her know we're here."

"Did she answer back?"

"Couldn't tell." He dove again. I kept a close watch on floating debris headed Dwight's way. The next time he came up he said, "I can't get in. See if you can find me something to break the window."

I double-checked that his rope was securely tied to the maple and searched for a rock. I wondered if breaking the window was a good idea. What if she was jammed inside, and he couldn't get her out?

A horn blaring from across the river diverted my attention. Also, someone was shouting my name. It sounded like in a dream when you hear things but can't respond. I didn't dare take my eyes from Dwight, nor divert my attention from the tenuous hold of the rope around my brother's waist.

Someone continued to call my name all the time Dwight was rapidly treading water to stay in place. When he gasped deeply, preparing to dive again, I looked in the direction of the calls. Across the river on the road at the foot of the hill was Lowell's pickup, gleaming red against the green background of leaves and the amber water whirling just inches in front of it. In his usual Western business suit, he was standing at water's edge, yelling and waving at us.

"Lowell!" I shouted.

"What's happened?"

"It's Shannon. The river . . ." I pointed to the front part of Shannon's car. I doubted that from his distance, he could see it under the water.

I was too far away to make out the expression on his face. But I saw his actions. Apparently he saw enough to recognize her car, for he plunged out on the bridge.

"No, you can't wade over. The current's too strong!" I shouted, waving my arms back and forth in a negative motion in case he couldn't hear me. "No, Lowell, don't!"

Up for air, Dwight yelled, "Don't try it, Lowell! Much too dangerous. I'll get her."

Lowell ignored both of us, but two steps into the current, he was down. If he hadn't grabbed the curbings and crawled back on his hands and knees, he would have been washed away. Branches, logs, and trash swept past us.

"Call for help!" I yelled. I knew he had a cell phone in his truck.

He was ahead of me on that. As soon as he reached his truck, he grabbed his phone. After making the 911 call, he clambered over boulders on the other side of the river to get as close to us as possible. He must have made a call to the store, because Chet was there

in minutes with more rope, and a hammer and
crowbar.

"I don't think she's hurt," Dwight said between
dives. "Both air bags inflated."

I waded out far enough to hand Dwight the tools.
"Be careful about breaking the window and flooding
the inside. Make sure you can get her out quickly."
We both knew I meant "before she drowns."

"Yeah, I know," Dwight said. "I won't break the
window until I can see how she is. I wish I could turn
the car right side up. Then I know I can get her out
on her side easily. The car won't budge. I tried." His
initial fright gone, he was thinking clearly now. He
worked methodically and carefully. I was still
trembling.

Across the river Lowell was studying how he could
get to us. "Throw me a rope," he shouted to Chet.

Rodeo-fashion, Chet tossed the rope. It fell short.
He threw several more times until Lowell caught the
loop and tied it high in a tree. Understanding what he
intended to do, Chet and I tied our end in a tree. Toss-
ing down his Stetson and removing his suit jacket,
bolo tie, and boots, Lowell clutched the line. He tested
it with his weight. It seemed taut enough. Then hand
over hand on the rope, stockinged feet held up as high
as he could hold them, but still dragging in the river,
Lowell made his way across.

Dwight, Chet, and I watched him walk his hands
along the rope. I was already terrified about Shannon
and worried about Dwight risking his life to save her.

Now Lowell was swinging like a monkey across the swollen river.

Chet put his hand on my shoulder. ''He'll make it. I seen him do it afore.''

When Lowell dropped beside me, I flew into his arms. He held me as if he'd never let me go. Chet clapped him on his back. Dwight's face showed the first signs of hope since Shannon disappeared in the flood.

''Hurry,'' Chet said.

''How did it happen?'' Lowell asked. ''She's an excellent driver and knows how to cross and when not to cross.''

''She made it across, but the approach washed out. She drove right into it.''

''Water's still risin'.'' Chet tapped Lowell to get his attention. He repeated, ''We better hurry.'' Chet hurried as fast as he could back to his shop for more tools to help us.

Lowell nodded.

Dwight was still in the river, trying unsuccessfully to pry the car upright with the crowbar. The log that stopped the downstream movement of the Cavalier was in his way. Next he tried using the log as the fulcrum point, but the crowbar slipped. Pieces of the log sloughed off.

''Is she hurt?'' Lowell's eyes begged me to say she was all right.

''We don't know.''

Lowell turned to Dwight. ''Can you see her?''

"No," Dwight said between deep intakes of breath, "but she's conscious. I can hear her tapping on something hard, probably the window. I keep banging on the car to let her know where I am. But hurry, man, we haven't much time. Water is seeping in now. It'll soon fill up."

Lowell waded in beside Dwight even before I could tie a rope to him. When he was beside Dwight, he gripped my brother in a half hug, partly, I know, to hold himself in place, but from the expression on his face, also with relief that Dwight was there.

Chet returned from his shop with more rope and a chain block and tackle. Dwight and Lowell tried righting the car, but even their combined strengths couldn't offset the current that forced the car back whenever they lifted it even slightly.

By diving and swimming around the car, Dwight fastened the chain around the right rear wheel. "When Lowell and I get set, I'll holler," he said to Chet when he came up for air. "You crank her up."

"Can't hear you under the water," Chet said.

I put one of Chet's ropes around my waist and handed him the end. "Wait until I get in there. I'll watch and give you the signal."

"Okay."

I said to Dwight, "Soon as the car is upright, you break the window and get the door opened. I'll pull Shannon out."

He nodded.

"Bring me that heavy stick," Lowell said.

Fighting the current, and staying as close to the bank as I could, I waded in beside Lowell. He held on to Dwight's rope to stay in place with one hand, and grasped the stick I brought in the other.

"Reckon her door is unlocked?" Chet asked. "It might be dangerous to break the window. Cut her face, or somethin'."

"No way it's unlocked," Lowell said. "I insist that she always keep it locked."

Dwight said, "Yeah, the car's locked. I tried the door right away."

"Hey, wait!" Lowell said. "I've got a key! We won't have to break a window." He dug in his pocket for his key ring and handed it to me. I ran though the bunch, easily recognizing the key for the Cavalier.

Funny what goes through your mind even in a life-and-death situation. First I wondered if the key remote would operate underwater. I clicked it, but of course, we didn't know if it worked. Then, as I held the key in my fingers ready to insert when the men righted the car, I thought about Lowell's obsession with crime. Even approaching a flooded river crossing and seeing us obviously in a dangerous position, Lowell had removed his heavy ring of keys from his pickup!

Dwight and Lowell dived. Lowell signaled they were ready. "Now!" I shouted to Chet.

Dwight with the crowbar and Lowell, using the stout stick, pried and lifted. Chet cranked on the pulley, tightening the chain. The car moved away from the log far enough to let the men get in better positions. Under them was the bedrock of the river. They had a solid support to pry against.

On the next dive, Dwight waved his hand over his head as a signal to me that they were ready. I was treading water above and beside them.

"Try again," I yelled to Chet.

He cranked. The car righted, stirring up some debris on the bottom. While the men surfaced to breathe, I ducked down in the water to the driver's door level. I couldn't see much. A dark shape, undoubtedly Shannon, was slumped in the seat. Her left palm was striking the window. When I pounded on it, she pressed her face against it. By getting at eye level on my side, I saw her lips moving.

"You okay?" I mouthed.

I couldn't make out what she said, lip-reading was too difficult through the muddy water and the poor light that reached the bottom of the river. But I could see she was in pain and crying.

I tried the door. It was locked. With fumbling fingers I inserted the key. When it caught and I turned it, I tried the latch again. It clicked. The door moved. Since I was on the downstream side of the Cavalier I wasn't fighting the current as the men had been in righting the car. When I opened the door a crack, the current helped me pull the door open all the way. Water swooped in.

Before the water completely covered Shannon, I felt her hands grabbing me. I tried to pull her out, but her seat belt held her. Dwight, reaching us as soon as he could dive after righting the car, quickly cut the belt with his knife. No longer able to hold my breath, I rose to the surface, gulped some air and went under again. Shannon had strangleholds on both Dwight and Lowell. Lowell gently scooted her from under the steering wheel that was pinning her in. Dwight held her legs. When they had firm holds on her, they nodded to each other and lifted her out. Safely free from the car, together they surfaced with her. Dwight carried her to the bank.

Even while choking, spitting up water, and sobbing with her arms almost strangling Dwight, Shannon kept looking back at Lowell. Her face drawn and deathly white, she watched Lowell struggle against the current. Without a rope around him as Dwight and I had and without having Dwight to hold on to, he was having difficulty holding his own against the current. Not until her brother crawled up onto the bank did she allow herself to lose consciousness.

Chapter Twelve

So used was I to the traffic noises from the interstate that at first I didn't pay any attention to the siren. But when it turned off on Highway M, I realized an ambulance was coming our way. Dwight, Lowell, Chet, and I were kneeling beside Shannon, who was lying on the rocky ground, just inches from the river. She was breathing rapidly. Her skin was cold and clammy.

When Maria ran down from the store carrying some quilts, we stepped back in relief, deferring to her first-aid training. She unbuttoned Shannon's blouse at the neck and wrapped a quilt around her. She ran her hands all over Shannon's body. When she touched her right ankle, Shannon groaned.

"Looks like she's broken her ankle," Maria said, "but I don't see anything else."

"Why isn't she conscious?" Lowell asked, wringing his hands. He stayed close to Shannon, moving back only when Maria came.

"From shock, fright, and pain."

Lowell knelt beside her, rubbing one of her hands in both of his. "Shannon, little sister, wake up. You're safe now. Open your eyes." Shannon made no response. "Please, Shannon, wake up."

Shannon's eyes opened. Her first expression was fright. Then, when she realized she where she was, she looked worried. She tried to rise as her blue eyes darted around until she focused on her brother. "Lowell," she murmured and closed her eyes again.

"No, Shannon, don't go to sleep. Stay awake," Maria said, patting her face. "Talk to us."

Shannon's eyes opened again with the same worried look. "Dwight?" she asked, the fright back in her expression.

"He's here, too," Lowell said, grabbing Dwight and bringing him into Shannon's vision.

"Hi," Dwight said. "You gave us a scare."

She looked at all of us crowded together leaning over her, including Bobby, Nora, Clyde, and Steve, who had arrived without any of us noticing.

"What happened?" Shannon asked. "I made it over the bridge, Lowell, just as you showed me how. Next thing I knew, I was lying on my side in the car turned over in the river. How did I that happen?"

"The road washed out," Lowell said. "You got across the bridge, but fell into a hole. But everything's okay now."

She held on to Lowell. "It was dark. I couldn't see and I couldn't move. My ankle..." She stiffled a scream when she tried to move it.

"You're safe now. Dwight saved you."

"Dwight," she reached for his hand, "I knew you were out there. I heard you knocking our special knock. Did you hear me knock back?"

"Yes," Dwight said, running his hand over her forehead to push back her long sandy-colored hair, "I heard." He knocked with his other hand on a nearby rock two times slowly, then three times in rapid succession. "Like that?"

"Yes. First it came from above me and then from everywhere. I couldn't tell where you were."

"I moved all around the car trying to let you know I was there."

"I kept going to sleep. I knew I shouldn't, so I moved my ankle, so the pain would keep me awake. I couldn't move, Dwight, but I wasn't so afraid anymore. I knew you were going to get me out." She took his hand from her forehead and held it.

"Paramedics are almost here," Chet said quietly to Lowell.

"And a wrecker," Nora said. She held Bobby close to her and spoke comforting words to him, so his mother could care for Shannon.

The ambulance, with its many-colored lights flashing, pulled up behind Lowell's pickup, which was blocking the bridge. The wrecker was right behind. Men piled out of both vehicles. Across the river, we saw the two paramedics and the driver of the wrecker gesturing and discussing what to do. They could see us all gathered around Shannon, who was lying on the bank wrapped in the colorful quilt.

As Clyde and I hurried up to the bridge where we could talk to the men, Clyde said, "River's crested and is already starting to fall. Fickle lady, this river. Moody and unpredictable."

"The approach is washed out. You can't get through!" I yelled to the men, pointing to the swirling pit of water in front of me where the road should be.

"Hi, Clyde," said one of the paramedics, "The call said Lowell Boyd's sister was involved. Anyone else?"

"No, just her, Weldon. She's conscious now, but in shock. Looks like she's broken her ankle."

The second paramedic saw the rope that Lowell had used to cross over still strung across the river.

"Will that rope hold me?" he asked.

"Lowell crossed over on it," I said. "If you can hang on, it will hold you."

"Good." He strapped on his medical kit, walked the far bank of the river to the tree, and as Lowell had done earlier, tested the rope's strength before crossing. Weldon, with other equipment, stayed on the other side, ready to return to the ambulance to get whatever supplies and equipment he needed.

I returned to Shannon when the paramedic reached her.

"Thanks, Eric, for getting here so quickly," Lowell

said, taking his medical kit as he dropped down from the rope.

"That's what we do. Can you rig up something to that rope so we can bring some equipment over here?"

"Sure, Chet and Dwight are already working on that."

Chet threw another rope across the river. "Grab hold, Weldon!" he yelled.

Dwight climbed the tree to fasten a pulley through the rope. He tied a tow rope to the pulley, leaving many feet dangling to stay on our side. With enough rope on each side of the river, the men could then pull the pulley back and forth.

"Now, yank it across," Chet hollered, holding the unused end of the tow rope.

Weldon pulled the pulley across. Chet played out his end. "Now," Chet said, "Tie your equipment to your end, and I'll run it over here."

While the men were rigging up the ropes and transporting the equipment, Eric, with Maria's assistance, worked on Shannon. He reassured Lowell about her condition. "Shock and a broken ankle. Plus a few bruises. I'll get her out of her shock. A trip to the emergency room to fix the ankle, and she'll be ready to come back home."

Lowell had stepped away while Eric was with Shannon. He stood close to me. "She'll be fine," I assured him. I put my hand on his arm.

"How can we get her back across the river?" Eric asked. "Is there any other road in here?"

"No. This is a dead end road," Lowell said. "Ends about a mile and a half at my place.

"You mean there's no other way across that river except that dangerous bridge?" He shook his head in amazement. "Looks like you'd have fixed that, being on the county court. I don't see how this girl kept from being killed. There's no other road?"

"No." I felt Lowell's body stiffen as he took hold of my hand on his arm and held it tight.

"Then how can we get her to the hospital? Or get the wrecker in here to pull her car out?" Now that Shannon was out of danger, we all looked at the sunken car. Already the blue of the front fender showed above water. Even I could see that the wrecker would have no trouble pulling the Cavalier out, if it could get across the river.

"You can cut through my field," Lowell said. "The back of my place borders the outer road. If you're careful and don't get stuck, you might be able to drive the ambulance and wrecker in that way. I've done it a few times with my four-wheel drive when the bridge was impassable. I think the ambulance can make it."

"We'll give it a try. I've been worse places. But you'll have to show us the way," Eric said.

"I can do that." Lowell didn't move. Instead his grip on me tightened.

"Go, man," Eric said, coming to us and physically turning Lowell around and pushing him toward the rope in the tree. He'd have to use the rope to get to his truck. "Your sister needs to get to a hospital as soon as possible to set this ankle.

"Maybe Dwight or I could go for you," I said when Lowell paused before climbing the tree to get back across the river. "You're too upset. We can do it."

"No, I have to do it. You don't know where you can drive without getting stuck. And I'll need to cut the fence to let them in. I must go."

"Lowell," Shannon said in a feeble voice. She tried to raise up to see him better. "Don't."

"He'll be all right, Miss Boyd," Eric said, holding her gently. "We can scoot him across with the pulley. All he has to do is hang on. Nothing to it."

"I'll be right back with the ambulance," Lowell reassured her, kissing her forehead. "Kay and Dwight will stay with you. They won't leave. I'll be back in a few minutes."

"Go," Eric said.

I handed Lowell his key ring. Chet ran a short rope through the pulley for Lowell to hold on to both ends. Chet signaled Weldon across the river to pull him across. In less than a minute, Lowell was standing on the rocky ledge across the river, putting his shoes and jacket back on. He waved to us, and he and Weldon hurried along the bank back to his truck.

Before he got behind the wheel, Lowell dug out a wooden box from the bed of his pickup and placed it in the middle of the road. He scrawled BRIDGE OUT on it.

The three vehicles backed up the narrow river ap-

proach until they could turn around. Following Lowell, the ambulance, its lights still on, the siren blaring
again, and the wrecker drove out of sight around the
bend.

Although we couldn't see them, we heard their pro-
gress as they turned left on to the outer road at the
access to the interstate. The siren let us track them as
they circled back, crossed the river on the outer road
and neared the rear of the Boyd Ranch acres. The
sound was stationary for a few minutes while Lowell
undoubtedly removed some fencing on his back field
for them to pass through. Then we heard the whine
move very slowly at first as they crossed the field, and
more rapidly when they reached the his driveway and
finally the gravel country road.

After Shannon was securely strapped on a board,
her ankle wrapped, I.V. and oxygen mask in place,
and made as comfortable as possible, Dwight, Weldon,
Chet, and Steve carried her to the front steps of my
store. The rest of us followed. We arrived there just
before Lowell and his entourage drove in from the
other direction.

When Shannon was in the ambulance, Lowell
started to climb in beside her. "No," he said to me,
changing his mind. "You go with her. Dwight and I
will follow."

He stepped into his pickup before he thought about
giving directions to the wrecker driver. He started to
get out when Steve said, "You go on, Lowell. Chet

and I will handle things here. We'll pull the Cavalier out.''

''Good. Tell him I'll come by tomorrow to see what the damage is.''

''Sure thing. You go on.''

Lowell motioned Dwight to get in beside him. ''The river will soon be down,'' he said to Steve, ''but there's still that washout in the fill. I'll call the graders to get here right away.'' He made a call from his truck right then. His message was succinct. He expected to be obeyed. ''They'll be here in an hour,'' he said to Steve. I'll send them in through my field. The road should be open by nightfall. That water spout upriver is about all spent. The river is falling fast.''

It was true. The water running now was almost back to its normal rate, just a few inches over the bridge, the big hole now visible.

Lowell waved his right hand at me directing me to ride with Shannon in the back of the ambulance. ''You're right, Kay. The bridge is dangerous. We'll do something about it.'' He had one foot in his pickup, but he stepped out again. He took me in his arms and looked long into my eyes. ''I love you, Kay.'' He kissed me in front of all the neighbors.

Over the buzzing in my ears and the rush of my heart, and over the roar of the river and the drone from the interstate, I heard clapping. When I looked around, Maria was grinning. Bobby was gawking at us with his mouth opened. Chet and Steve slapped a youthful high-five. Nora and Clyde put their arms around each other. Dwight gave a "Yahoo," and then whistled.

Then Lowell jumped into his truck beside Dwight and led off again, the ambulance behind.

Here I was front and center again, when the spotlight should be on Shannon. Embarrassed, but grinning, I sat beside Shannon. She looked much better already. Of all the people there in the road in front of my Merryman's Store, including the driver of the wrecker, she was the only one who didn't see Lowell kiss me.

"Where's Lowell?" she asked. "And Dwight? Are they all right? Did they get hurt with all their diving?"

"They are fine. No, they didn't get hurt. Just wet, and they are already dry in this heat. And don't you worry about them hating each other anymore. They are up there ahead of us sitting side by side in Lowell's pickup."

Shannon smiled.

"And Lowell asked Dwight to ride with him."

"I knew he'd come around," Shannon said.

We turned onto the Boyd Ranch driveway and paused a bit for Dwight to open the gate at the barn. We drove through and waited for him to close it. We went through two other gates, including the paddock where Shannon's mare was. Shannon smiled as she watched her mare follow along, curious about this strange vehicle. Then the ambulance lurched over the rough field. When we reached the outer road, Lowell and Dwight got out to direct Weldon as he steered it down into the ditch and up the other side to reach the pavement. With no sirens, but lights flashing, the ambulance led the way as we merged into the traffic at the interstate on our way to the hospital in town twenty miles away.

Shannon was looking better all the time. Color was back in her face. The effects of her shock were wearing off, and the injection Eric gave her numbed her ankle pain. She lifted up her head from the pillow enough to see out the back window of the ambulance that the red pickup was following closely. Its tall driver, wearing a white, slightly soiled Stetson hat was gesturing amiably to the younger man sitting next to him.

"Finally," Shannon said, as she lay back, a satisfied grin on her face. "I knew they'd both come around."

I waved out the window to both of them. They were too engrossed in their conversation to see me. I guess I was smiling happily because Shannon looked long at me. "You know, Kay, Lowell really likes you."

"Yes, I know."

"I mean really, really likes you." Shannon grabbed my hand. "He's never had anyone he's gone with more than a few times. He's always been so dedicated, such a sense of duty. To the ranch. But mostly it was to me. Then when I got older he sort of eased up on that. Now he's really into this county commissioner gig. He likes it and is good at it. I think he'll go for other public offices later."

"He'd make a great senator."

"The best. Then he could clean up really big crimes."

We laughed.

"And build bridges all over the state?" She giggled.

"He just now said that he was going to build a better bridge at Merryman's Crossing."

"No kidding?"

"That's right."

"Well, it took a near-drowning to convince him."

When Shannon's ankle was set (it was not a major break but a hairline fracture) and everything else checked out all right, she was released to go home. We borrowed Dad's car, so she could have the whole backseat to support her leg. Dwight and I planned to drive her home.

Lowell said, "I've been in touch with the graders, and they have the road repaired. We can go over the bridge." He turned to Dwight. "Can you drive her home by yourself?"

"Sure." Dwight was surprised.

"Sorry I was so hard on you, man. Perhaps I acted hastily."

Dwight didn't say, "That's all right," because what Lowell did to him wasn't all right. He stood there looking at Lowell, not saying anything.

Lowell seemed nervous, but he continued his apology. "The judge said no young person who had the same restrictions set on him as you did has ever paid off a fine so quickly. In less than three months! He was impressed. So am I."

Dwight still didn't say anything. I thought to myself that if Lowell had taken the trouble to look into the situation more closely, he would have seen Dwight's quality and capabilities. That one incident was a fluke. Not worth ruining his life over. But then, I was prejudiced.

Lowell held out his hand to Dwight. "I'm proud to shake your hand. I can never repay you for saving my sister's life."

That Dwight could respond to. "We both did that. With Kay's and Chet's help. I couldn't have done it by myself." They shook hands. Shannon and I exchanged grateful glances. Our relations with these two men would be much easier now.

Before Shannon and Dwight left, I leaned into the backseat to see if Shannon was comfortable. Intending to spread it over her legs, I picked up the quilt folded neatly by the orderly and placed on the seat beside her.

"Where did this come from?" I asked in surprise. And admiration. It was a handsewn quilt.

"That's one of the covers Maria brought out of the store to put on me at the river," Shannon said. "Why?"

I held up a corner to look more closely. The small blocks of prints and solids melded together, the pastel colors with brighter ones. Intertwining patterns of loops covered the entire top that was quilted with tiny stitches. The last time I saw Grandma, she was propped up in her chair in the store, putting the finishing touches to the binding on this quilt.

Lowell leaned over me to see what I was doing. "Grandma's last quilt," I said, showing it to him. "Maria must have found it when we needed something to cover Shannon there on the river bank." I ran my hands over the surface, admiring it. The quilt didn't make me sad; it only helped me remember happy times. "I wonder where she found it."

"Where she always kept her quilts she was working on," Lowell said, "under the seat in that bench in the library section. Haven't you looked in there?"

"No. I didn't realize the seat opened up."

"All the neighbors knew that," Shannon said. "We often saw Faith put her work away when we came in the store. Maria knew where to find a cover in a hurry." She spread the quilt out over her lap. It's sure pretty. What's the name of the pattern, I wonder?"

"The Wedding Ring." I didn't tell them that Grandma had shown it to me on that last visit. I had forgotten about that. Her hand had shaked as she pointed to different blocks that included pieces from my dresses I wore when I was little.

"It's one of my favorite patterns," Grandma had said. "The Wedding Ring." Grandpa had come over to us when his customer left and put his arm over her shoulder. She moved her head, so her cheek touched his hand. "See, now, Olen, I've finished it." She and Grandpa exchanged one of their glances and then both smiled at me.

Lowell's arm was around my shoulders as we watched Shannon and Dwight drive off. I tilted my head against him, the hairs on his arm tickling my face. It was the most natural thing in the world for us to walk together toward his pickup.

Since their death, I had never felt the presence of my grandparents more than on the drive home while I was sitting close by Lowell. Remembering them caused me to smile. Besides assuring that the store would continue, and somehow arranging matters so that Lowell and Dwight could set things straight between them, they also played Cupid. Merl and Vivian got married, Dwight could now date Shannon, and Lowell and I?

Did they have us in mind when they finagled it so that we had to work together at the schoolhouse? Or when Grandma made her last quilt?

I put my hand on Lowell's leg. He covered it with his and squeezed, shooting me a swift, pleased grin before he had to focus on the heavy evening traffic of the interstate. An electric surge of delight flowed through me. Now I had everything—my family, my store, good neighbors, my writing. And Lowell.

Together we drove back to Merryman's Crossing, one of Missouri's dying towns whose citizens refused to let die.